全新！NEW GEPT

全民英檢

中級

寫作&口說 題庫解析

新制修訂版

語言中心委員會、郭文興、陳鈺璽—— 著

全書 MP3 一次下載

9789864541775.zip

「此為 zip 壓縮檔，請先安裝解壓縮程式或 APP，
iOS 系統請升級至 iOS 13 後再行下載，
此為大型檔案，建議使用 WIFI 連線下載以免占用流量，
並確認連線狀況，以利下載順暢。」

全民英語能力分級檢定測驗的問與答

財團法人語言訓練中心（LTTC）自 2000 年全民英檢（General English Proficiency Test, GEPT）推出至今，持續進行該測驗可信度及有效度的研究，以期使測驗品質最佳化。

因此，自 2021 年一月起，GEPT 調整部分初級、中級及中高級的聽讀測驗題數與題型內容，並提供成績回饋服務。另一方面，此次調整主要目的是要反映 108 年國民教育新課綱以「素養」及「學習導向評量（Learning Oriented Assessment）」為中心的教育理念，希望可以透過適當的測驗內容與成績回饋，有效促進國人的英語溝通能力。而調整後的題型與內容將更貼近日常生活，且更能符合各階段英文學習的歷程。透過適當的測驗內容與回饋，使學生更有效率地學習與應用。

Q 本項測驗在目的及性質方面有何特色？

整體而言，有四項特色：

(1)本測驗的對象包含在校學生及一般社會人士，測驗目的在評量一般英語能力（general English proficiency），命題不侷限於特定領域或教材；

(2)整套系統共分五級--初級(Elementary)、中級(Intermediate)、中高級(High-Intermediate)、高級(Advanced)、優級(Superior)—根據各階段英語學習者的特質及需求，分別設計題型及命題內容，考生可依能力選擇適當等級報考；

(3)各級測驗均重視聽、說、讀、寫四種能力的評量；

(4)本測驗係「標準參照測驗」(criterion-referenced test)，每級訂有明確的能力指標，考生只要通過所報考級數即可取得該級的合格證書。

Q 「全民英檢」與美國的「托福測驗」(TOEFL)、英國的測驗(如 FCE或IELTS)有何不同？

IELTS的性質與TOEFL類似，對象均是擬赴英語系國家留學的留學生，內容均與校園生活與學習情境有關，因此並不一定適合國內各階段英語學習者。FCE則是英國劍橋大學研發的英語檢定測驗中的一級，在內容方面未必符合國內英語教學目標及考生生活經驗。

其實近年來，日本及中國大陸均已研發自己的英語能力分級測驗，日本有STEP測驗，中國大陸則有PET及CET等測驗。由此可見，發展本土性的英語能力分級測驗實為時勢所趨。

Q 本測驗既包含聽、說、讀、寫四項，各項測驗方式為何？

聽力及閱讀測驗採選擇題方式，口說及寫作測驗則採非選擇題方式，每級依能力指標設計題型。以中級為例，聽力部分含35題，作答時間約30分鐘；閱讀部分含35題，作答時間45分鐘；寫作部分

含中翻英、引導寫作,作答時間40分鐘;口說測驗採錄音方式進行,作答時間約15分鐘。

⒬ 這項測驗各級命題方向為何?考生應如何準備?

全民英檢在設計各級的命題方向時,均曾參考目前各級英語教育之課程大綱,同時也廣泛搜集相關教材進行內容分析,以求命題內容能符合國內各級英語教育的需求。同時,為了這項測驗的內容能反應本土的生活經驗與特色,因此命題內容力求生活化,並包含流行話題及時事。

由於這項測驗並未針對特定領域或教材命題,考生應無需特別準備。但因各級測驗均包含聽、說、讀、寫四部分,而目前國內英語教育仍偏重讀與寫,因此考生必須平日加強聽、說訓練,同時多接觸英語媒體(如報章雜誌、廣播、電視、電影等),以求在測驗時有較好的表現。

⒬ 口說及寫作測驗既採非選擇題方式,評分方式為何?

口說及寫作測驗的評分工作將由受過訓練的專業人士擔任,每位考生的表現都會經過至少兩人的評分。每級口說及寫作測驗均訂有評分指標,評分人員在確切掌握評分指標後,依據考生的整體表現評分。

⒬ 通過「全民英檢」合格標準者是否取得合格證書?又合格證書有何用途或效力?

是的，通過「全民英檢」合格標準者將頒給證書。以目前初步的規畫，全民英檢測驗之合格證明書能成為民眾求學或就業的重要依據，同時各級學校也可利用本測驗做為學習成果檢定及教學改進的參考。

Ｑ 全民英檢測驗的分數如何計算？

初試各項成績採標準計分方式，60分為平均數，每一標準差加減20分，滿分120分。初試兩項測驗成績總和達160分，且其中任一項成績不低於72分者，始可參加複試。如以傳統粗分計分概念來說，聽力測驗每題2.67分，閱讀測驗每題3分，各項得分為答對題數乘上每題分數，可以大概計算是否通過本項測驗。實際計分方式會視當次考生程度與試題難易作調整，因此每題分數及最高分與粗分計分方式略有差異。複試各項成績採整體式評分，使用級分制，分為0~5級分，再轉換成百分制。複試各項成績均達八十分以上，視為通過。

Ｑ 採標準計分方式有何優點？

考生不會受不同次測驗中考生程度與試題難易之影響。

Ｑ 國中、高中學生若無國民身分證，如何報考？

國中生未請領身分證者，可使用印有相片之健保IC卡影本替代；高中生以上中華民國國民請使用國民身分證正面影本。外籍人士需備有效期限內之台灣居留證影本。

PRELUDE

Q 初試與複試一定在同一考區嗎？

測驗中心原則上會儘量安排在同一地區，但初試、複試借用的考區不盡相同，故複試的考場一律由測驗中心安排。

Q 請問合格證書的有效期限只有兩年嗎？

合格證書並無有效期限，而是成績紀錄保存兩年，意即兩年內的成績單，如因故遺失，可申請補發。成績單申請費用100元，證書300元，申請表格備索。

Q 複試是否在一天內結束？

不一定，視考生人數而定，確定的時間以複試准考証所載之測驗時間為準。

Q 報考全民英檢是否有年齡、學歷的限制？

除國小生外。本測驗適合台灣地區之英語學習者報考。

Q 合格之標準為何？

初試兩項測驗成績總和達160分，且其中任一項成績不低於72分者，複試成績除初級寫作為70分，其餘級數的寫作、口說測驗都80分以上才算通過，可獲核發合格證書。

Q 初試通過，複試未通過，下一次是否還需要再考一次初試？

初試通過者，可於二年內單獨報考複試未通過項目。

Q 考生可申請單項合格證書

另外，證書核發也有新制，除了現在已經有的「聽讀證書」與「聽讀說寫證書」外，也可以申請口說或寫作的單項合格證書，方便考生證明自己的英語強項，更有利升學、求職。

★關於「全民英語能力分級檢定測驗」之內容及相關問題請洽：

財團法人語言訓練測驗中心

中心地址：106台北市辛亥路二段170號 (台灣大學校總區內)

郵政信箱：台北郵政第 23-41號信箱

電話：(02)2362-6385~7

傳真：(02)2367-1944

辦公日：週一至週五(週六、日及政府機構放假日不上班)

辦公時間：上午八點至十二點、下午一點至五點

CONTENTS

目錄

NEW GEPT
全新!全民英檢中級 寫作&口說題庫解析

全民英檢複試應考當天的注意事項

☆當天所須攜帶的物件

□有效身分證件：中華民國身分證（或有效期限內的護照、駕照）正本。國中生可用：中華民國身分證、有效期限內的護照正本、印有相片之健保IC卡正本。外籍人士可用：有效期內的台灣居留證正本。）

□准考證

□普通黑色鉛筆或藍／黑色原子筆、橡皮擦、修正液

☆當天應試前的準備與注意事項

1. 以鉛筆作答者，請準備兩枝以上削尖的鉛筆或自動筆，因為考試開始後不可能有時間做削鉛筆的動作。以原子筆作答者，請準備兩枝以上的黑／藍色原子筆，並事先確認不會中途斷水，以防止因沒水而無法完成考試。

2. 務必提早到考場，給自己充裕時間確認貼在入口處／走廊上自己的考試教室與座位，以及做考前的複習。以免在快到測驗的時間時，不但要跟別的考生擠著確認自己的教室／座位，若遇到特殊情況（例如當天臨時換教室）也沒有足夠的時間應對。

3. 在測驗教室前排隊等候時，請利用時間保持英文思考的環境。一般到了考試現場，許多考生的習慣往往就是開始用中文聊天，這其實很扼殺自己的考試能力，因為在寫作／口說測驗中，直接以英文的思考邏輯來答題，表達出來的內容才最為流暢。因此，建議在入場前閱讀（或朗讀）英文的文章、句子，也可以聽英文廣播，來掌握英文的思考結構與流暢度。

4. 在進入考場之前，先把有效證件、准考證，以及相關文具都先準備好，取消所有電子儀器的鬧鈴設定，並將手機的電池取出，以便於入場後能迅速將不需帶入座位之物品擺至測驗教室的前方地板上，並馬上找到自己的座位。

5. 為了讓口說測驗順利作答，在正式考試前考務人員會要求你檢查錄音設備，此時務必詳細檢查你的耳機、錄音設備是否都正常，而且不會干擾到你的答題，否則因錄音設備而影響到考試成績，是很冤枉的。

第一回　寫作能力測驗答題注意事項

1. 本測驗共有兩部分。第一部分為中譯英，第二部分為英文作文。測驗時間為 **40 分鐘**。

2. 請利用試題紙空白處背面擬稿，但正答務必書寫在「寫作能力測驗答案紙」上。在答案紙以外的地方作答，不予計分。

3. 第一部分中譯英請在答案紙第一頁作答，第二部分英文作文請在答案紙第二頁作答。

4. 作答時請勿隔行書寫，請注意字跡清晰可讀，並保持答案紙之清潔，以免影響評分。

5. 測驗時，不得在准考證或其他物品上抄題，亦不得有傳遞、夾帶小抄、左顧右盼或交談等違規行為。

6. 意圖或已經將試題紙攜出試場者，五年內不得報名參加本測驗。請人代考者，連同代考者，三年內不得報名參加本測驗。

7. 測驗結束時，須立即停止作答，在原位靜候監試人員收回全部試題紙及答案紙，清點無誤後，宣佈結束始可離場。

8. 應試者入場、出場及測驗中如有違反上列規則或不服監試人員之指示者，監試人員得取消應試資格並請其離場，且作答不予計分。

全民英語能力分級檢定測驗

中級寫作能力測驗

本測驗共有兩部份。第一部份為中譯英，第二部份為英文寫作。測驗時間為 40 分鐘。

一、中譯英 (40%)

說明：請將下列的一段中文翻譯成通順、達意且前後連貫的英文。

> 找工作的傳統方式是看報紙的分類廣告。然而，隨著科技的發達，網路早就已經成為求職的主要管道。公司和僱主可以把工作職缺刊登在公司的網頁上，無須再花費一毛錢登報。求職者也可以在網路上張貼他們的履歷。

二、英文作文 (60%)

請依下面所提供的文字提示寫一篇英文作文，長度約 120 字（8 至 12 個句子）。作文可以是一個完整的段落，也可以分段。（評分重點包括內容、組織、文法、用字遣詞、標點符號、大小寫。）

> 提示：近幾年來飲食安全的問題經常登上新聞頭條，有些廠商為了降低成本謀取暴利而採用劣等食材，部分原料對人體是有害的。你認為有什麼方法能夠杜絕這些不良廠商的惡劣行為？你認為消費者是要自己提高警覺，還是有關當局必須採取某些防範措施？

第一部份請由第 1 行開始作答，請勿隔行書寫。　　　　第 1 頁

25

30

35

40

第一回　口說能力測驗答題注意事項

1. 本測驗問題由耳機播放，回答則經麥克風錄下。分朗讀短文、回答問題與看圖敘述三部分，時間共約 15 分鐘，連同口試說明時間共需約五十分鐘。

2. 第一部份朗讀短文有 1 分鐘準備時間，此時請勿唸出聲音，待聽到「請開始朗讀」2 分鐘的朗讀時間開始時，再將短文唸出來。第二部分回答問題的題目將播出 2 遍，聽完第二次題目後要立即回答。第三部份看圖敘述有 30 秒的思考時間及 1 分 30 秒的答題時間，思考時不可在試題紙上作記號，亦不可出聲。等聽到指示開始回答時，請您針對圖片盡量的回答。

3. 錄音設備皆已事先完成設定，請勿觸動任何機件，以免影響錄音。測驗時請戴妥耳機，將麥克風調到嘴邊約三公分處，聽清楚說明，依指示以適中音量回答。

4. 評分人員將根據您錄下的回答（發音與語調、語法與字彙、可解度及切題度等）作整體的評分。您可利用所附光碟自行測試，一一錄下回答後，再播出來聽聽，並斟酌調整。練習時請盡量以英語思考、應對，考試時較易有自然的表現。

5. 請注意測試時不可在試題紙上劃線、打「√」或作任何記號；不可在准考證或其他物品上抄題；亦不可有傳遞、夾帶小抄、左顧右盼或交談等違規行為。

6. 意圖或已將試題紙或試題影音資料攜出或傳送出試場者，視同侵犯本中心著作財產權，限五年內不得報名參加「全民英檢」測驗。請人代考，連同代考者，三年內不得報名參加本測驗。

7. 測驗結束時，須立即停止作答，在原位靜候監試人員收回全部試題紙且清點無誤後，等候監試人員宣布結束後始可離場。

8. 入場、出場及測驗中如有違反規則或不服監試人員指示者，監試人員將取消您的應試資格並請您離場，且作答不予計分，亦不退費。

全民英語能力分級檢定測驗

中級口說能力測驗

請在 15 秒內完成並唸出下列自我介紹的句子：

My seat number is （座位號碼後 5 碼）, and my registration number is （考試號碼後 5 碼）.

第一部分：朗讀短文

　　請先利用 1 分鐘的時間閱讀下面的短文，然後在 2 分鐘內以正常的速度，清楚正確的讀出下面的短文，閱讀時請不要發出聲音。

　　Here are some tips on job interviews. First and foremost, familiarize yourself with the questions frequently asked during interviews and prepare the answers beforehand according to your situation. Second, dress decently and formally. Remember to practice smiling at yourself in the mirror to look confident. Finally, keep in mind that honesty is the best policy.

*　　　　　*　　　　　*

　　Today was my first day at work. My supervisor left me by myself after he explained my job responsibilities and duties to me. I realized that I didn't fully understand what I was supposed to do. Instead of making mistakes, I decided to ask the coworkers around me for help. Fortunately, they were all very friendly. I believe that given some time, I will be able to handle my job alone.

第二部分：回答問題

　　共十題。題目已事先錄音，每題經由耳機播出二次，不印在試卷上。第一至五題，每題回答時間 15 秒；第六至十題，每題回答時間 30 秒。每題播出後，請立即回答。回答時，不一定要用完整的句子，但請在作答時間內儘量的表達。

第三部分：看圖敘述

　　下面有一張圖片及四個相關的問題，請在一分半鐘內完成作答。作答時，請直接回答，不需將題號及題目唸出。

　　首先請利用 30 秒的時間看圖及問題。

提示：
1. 照片裡的人在什麼地方？
2. 照片裡的人在做什麼？
3. 照片裡的人為什麼會在那裡？
4. 如果尚有時間，請詳細描述圖片中的景物。

請將下列自我介紹的句子再唸一遍：

My seat number is（座位號碼後 5 碼）, and my registration number is
（考試號碼後 5 碼）.

複試 寫作測驗 解析

第一部分 **中譯英** (40%)

請將下列的一段中文翻譯成通順、達意且前後連貫的英文。

找工作的傳統方式是看報紙的分類廣告。然而，隨著科技的發達，網路早就已經成為求職的主要管道。公司和僱主可以把工作職缺刊登在公司的網頁上，無須再花費一毛錢登報。求職者也可以在網路上張貼他們的履歷。

The traditional way of looking for a job is to look up the classified ads in the newspaper. However, with the advance in technology, the Internet has become the main avenue for seeking employment. Companies and employers can advertise job vacancies on their websites, without having to spend a single cent on newspaper ads. Job seekers can likewise post their résumés on the Internet.

逐句說明

1. 找工作的傳統方式是看報紙的分類廣告。

The traditional way of looking for a job is to look up the classified ads in the newspaper.

中譯英最重要的一點就是要有足夠的單字量來應付，因為不夠的話就會遇到你不知道該用什麼單字去翻譯的狀況，例如平常不知道「分類廣告」的英文是「classified ads」，第一個句子就無法順利完成。本句其實很簡單，是用標準的「A is B」（A 是 B）的句型寫成，不過要注意 is 後面的補語部分，後面不能直接用原形「look up」，而是要轉變成不定詞的「to look up」，避免一個句子裡出現兩個動詞。還要注意不要因為中文是「報紙上」就錯譯成「on the newspaper」，正確的說法是「in the newspaper」。

18

第 1 回

第 2 回

第 3 回

第 4 回

第 5 回

第 6 回

2. 然而，隨著科技的發達，網路早就已經成為求職的主要管道。

However, with the advance in technology, the Internet has become the main avenue for seeking employment.

「隨著科技的發達 with the advance in technology」這句表達很常見，可以直接記下來。「已經成為」顯然是完成式的時態，因此要用「has become」。avenue 指的是人們在路上走走的街道，但也可以用來表示做某事的「管道」。另外，網路 Internet 的第一個字母要大寫，前面的定冠詞 the 也不要忘記要加上去。

3. 公司和僱主可以把工作職缺刊登在公司的網頁上，無須再花費一毛錢登報。

Companies and employers can advertise job vacancies on their websites, without having to spend a single cent on newspaper ads.

「把…刊登」是本句的主要動詞，受詞是「工作職缺」，所以翻譯成英文時要把順序回復成「動詞+受詞」，本句「把工作職缺刊登」用英文表達就要轉換成「刊登工作職缺 advertise job vacancies」的順序。「無須，沒有，不用做…」可以用 without V-ing 的句型，例如：You can do online shopping without leaving your home.（你無須出門，就可以在網路上購物）。

4. 求職者也可以在網路上張貼他們的履歷。

Job seekers can likewise post their résumés on the Internet.

當遇到中文的「也」時，翻譯時除了可以用 too 或 also，也可以試著用 likewise 等詞彙來替換，換用不一樣的單字，而非一直重複使用那幾個常見的單字，閱卷老師可能會對你比較有印象而多給分。中文的習慣會把地點、時間副詞片語放在動作的前面，所以「在網路」會在「貼上」的前面，但英文習慣把地方、時間副詞片語放在句尾，所以 on the Internet 放在最後。Internet 可寫成 Net，雖然 Net 是簡稱，第一個字母還是要記得大寫喔！

19

> 請依下面所提供的文字提示寫一篇英文作文，長度約 120 字（8 至 12 個句子）。作文可以是一個完整的段落，也可以分段。

 近幾年來飲食安全的問題經常登上新聞頭條，有些廠商為了降低成本謀取暴利而採用劣等食材，部分原料對人體是有害的。你認為有什麼方法能夠杜絕這些不良廠商的惡劣行為？你認為消費者是要自己提高警覺，還是有關當局必須採取某些防範措施？

結構預設

本題主要是針對食安的問題提出自己的意見。一開始可以先從「有關當局必須採取防範措施」來破題，進而提出「防範」及「杜絕」的措施有哪些。

草稿擬定

1. 杜絕不良廠商的方法有：重罰（heavy fines、harsher punishments），加強稽查（more frequent inspections），內部指控（workers who expose、accusations from workers、whistle-blower）

2. 消費者要提高警覺（customers should beware of...）：仔細閱讀成分標示（read the contents label carefully），不要食用顏色、味道奇怪的食品（don't consume the foods with strange colors, smells and tastes）

3. 有關當局必須採取防範措施（the authorities concerned should take precautions to...）：制定更嚴格的法律（make stricter laws），加強食品來源管理及流向追蹤（enhance food source management and traceability）

作文範例

I think that the government has to ①come up with concrete measures to deal with the root of the problem. Food manufacturers ignored ②the health of the public and violated clearly-established regulations. ③Fines alone might not work as they are insignificant to companies that make billions of dollars. Mixing harmful components into the food supply should be ④viewed as a serious crime, and offenders should be

⑤sentenced to five to ten years in prison, ⑥apart from heavy fines. ⑦Factories found with such ingredients should be shut down immediately. ⑧Perhaps we should offer a reward to workers who expose the evil deeds of food manufacturers. ⑨In addition, more manpower and funds should be allocated to the health department.

範例中譯

我認為政府必須想出具體的措施來處理問題的根源。食品製造商忽略大眾的健康並違反明文規定的條例。單憑罰款可能沒有作用，因為罰款對於賺幾十億的公司而言是微不足道的。在食物供應中混入有害的成分應該被視為一項嚴重的犯罪，而觸犯者應被判五至十年的有期徒刑，除了鉅額罰款以外。被發現擁有這些原料的工廠應立刻被迫關閉。或許我們應該提供獎賞給揭發食品製造商惡行的員工。此外，也應該分配更多的人力和經費給衛生局。

重點文法分析

① come up with 指「想出辦法」，另一種表達方式是 think of ways to。

② 台灣的「健保制度」可翻譯為 the public healthcare system，而「民眾的健康」是 the health of the public，可以把介系詞 of 看作「…的…」的意思，例如前任美國總統林肯的著名演講： the government of the people, by the people, for the people（政府應是民有、民治、民享）。

③ N alone might not V（單憑…本身或許無法…），這種句型在提出觀點時非常實用，建議可以在報告或會議中使用。

例句 Punishment alone might not solve bullying problems in schools.

單憑處罰或許解決不了校園霸凌的問題。

例句 Advertisements alone might not increase sales.

單憑廣告或許無法增加銷售額。

④ 「某人把某件事視為」，「某事件被視為」，英文用被動語態 be + p.p.，除了用 be viewed as，也可以用 be considered 或 be seen as。

例句 Golf is considered a sport for the rich and famous.

高爾夫球被視為是有錢人和名人的運動。

⑤ 「被判有期徒刑…年」的英文是 sentenced to ... years in prison，「無期徒刑」是 life sentence，「死刑」是 death sentence，「假釋」是 go on parole。

⑥ 英文有兩種涵義的「除此之外」，一種是有包括之前提到的事情，可理解為「除了…還有」，例如：besides、in addition to、apart from 和 other than。另一種「除此之外」則不包含之前提到的事情，可理解為「除了…例外」，例如：except、but for 和 save for 兩者之間的差異可以參考以下例子。

例句 I go to school every day besides Monday to Friday.
我每天去學校，除了星期一到星期五，還有星期六、日。

例句 I go to school every day except on Saturday and Sunday.
我每天去學校，除了星期六和星期日例外。

⑦ 判斷該用主動語態或被動語態的關鍵，是先找出動詞，然後判斷主詞是否有「做出」某個動作，還是「被…」的狀態。
若用主動語態，表示工廠發現這些原料，是工廠主動有「found 發現」的動作。仔細想想，發現工廠有這些原料的應該是人，不是工廠，因此這句話要用被動語態 be + p.p.：Factories (that are) found with such ingredients should be shut down immediately.。同樣的，工廠不會主動有「shut down 關閉」的動作，工廠是被關閉的。使用被動語態主要是強調主動語態中的受詞，例如句子中的工廠原本是受詞，在被動語態中變成了主詞。至於做出「found 發現」和「shut down 關閉」這些動作的人因為不是強調的重點，可以完全省略。

⑧ 這句需要注意的第一個地方是 offer something to someone（提供某東西給某人），介系詞用 to。第二要注意的地方是關係代名詞 who。關係代名詞也是代名詞，who 是代替「人」的主格代名詞，which 代替「物」的主格代名詞。工人當然是人，所以用 who 代替 they。若不確定該用何者，可用關係代名詞 that 來取代 who 和 which。

⑨ 寫作文需要有充足的副詞字彙量，例如中文的「此外、再者、更何況」，若之前已經用了 In addition，在後面的句子則可改用 moreover 或 furthermore。

複試 口說測驗 解析

▶▶▶ 第一部分 朗讀短文

請先利用 1 分鐘的時間閱讀下面的短文，閱讀時請不要發出聲音，
然後在 2 分鐘內以正常的速度，清楚正確的讀出下面的短文。

 短文

Here are some tips on job interviews. First and foremost, familiarize yourself with the questions frequently asked during interviews and prepare the answers beforehand according to your situation. Second, dress decently and formally. Remember to practice smiling at yourself in the mirror to look more confident. Finally, keep in mind that honesty is the best policy.

*　　　　　　　*　　　　　　　*

Today was my first day at work. My supervisor left me by myself after he explained my job responsibilities and duties to me. I realized that I didn't fully understand what I was supposed to do. Instead of making mistakes, I decided to ask the coworkers around me for help. Fortunately, they were all very friendly. I believe that given some time, I will be able to handle my job alone.

中譯

這裡有一些工作面試方面的建議。首先，讓自己熟悉一些在面試時經常被問到的問題，並依照自己的情況事先準備好答案。第二，穿著要得體且正式。記得在鏡子前練習對自己微笑，以便看起來更有自信。最後，切記誠實以對是最好的對策。

*　　　　　　　*　　　　　　　*

今天是我第一天上班。我的主管在解釋工作職責後，就讓我自己一個人工作。我發現我並沒有完全明白我應該要做什麼事情。與其犯錯，我決定向我身邊的同事尋求協助。幸好，他們都很友善。我相信只要給我一些時間，我就能獨自處理我的工作。

高分解析

1 重要單字：interview [ˋɪntəˏvju] 面試；foremost [ˋforˏmost] 最重要的；familiarize [fəˋmɪljəˏraɪz] 使熟悉；frequently [ˋfrɪkwəntlɪ] 頻繁地；decently [ˋdisn̩tlɪ] 合適地；honesty [ˋɑnɪstɪ] 誠實；supervisor [ˏsupəˋvaɪzə] 指導者，主管；explain [ɪkˋsplen] 解釋；responsibility [rɪˏspɑnsəˋbɪlətɪ] 責任；suppose [səˋpoz] 猜想，以為；fortunately [ˋfɔrtʃənɪtlɪ] 幸運地；handle [ˋhændl̩] 應付；處理。

2 請注意 tips、mistakes 最後的 s 要發[s]音，因為前面為無聲子音。interviews、questions、answers、responsibilities、duties、coworkers 則要發[z]，因為前面為有聲子音或母音。請務必習慣正確唸出英文的複數形，不要忽略不發音。

3 **朗讀高分技巧**
多數英語學習者在說英文的時候都缺乏英文應有的抑揚頓挫，造成語氣平淡，聽起來就會缺乏活力和自信。一個句子中總會有一些單字需要強調，以下朗讀文章中有顏色的單字需要唸稍微大聲一點，讓語調有起伏。另外，斷句也是一個很重要的技巧。有些比較長的句子，若完全不停頓一口氣匆匆念完，反而會扣分。文章中有 | 的地方表示可以稍做停頓，讓語氣更加從容、更有自信。

Here are some tips | on job interviews. | First and foremost, | familiarize yourself | with the questions frequently asked during interviews | and prepare the answers beforehand | according to your situation. | Second, | dress decently and formally. | Remember to practice | smiling at yourself in the mirror | to look more confident. | Finally, | keep in mind that honesty | is the best policy.

第 1 回
第 2 回
第 3 回
第 4 回
第 5 回
第 6 回

*   *   *

Today was my first day at work. | My supervisor left me by myself | after he explained my job responsibilities | and duties to me. | I realized | that I didn't fully understand | what I was supposed to do. | Instead of making mistakes, | I decided to ask the coworkers around me | for help. | Fortunately, | they were all very friendly. | I believe that given some time, | I will be able | to handle my job alone.

▶▶▶ 第二部分 回答問題

> 這個部分共有 10 題。題目已事先錄音，每題經由耳機播出二次，不印在試卷上。第 1 至 5 題，每題回答時間 15 秒；第 6 至 10 題，每題回答時間 30 秒。每題播出後，請立即回答。回答時，不一定要用完整的句子，但請在作答時間內儘量的表達。

1 **What are your plans for the coming weekend?**

你對即將到來的週末假期有什麼計畫？

答題策略

1. 問週末有什麼計畫，如果沒有計畫，可以如實的說「沒有計畫」，但還是要講一些週末可能會做的事情，絕對不能簡單的說 I don't have any plans. 就等著下一題，雖然這樣也算是回答了問題，但要知道這一部分的答題時間少則 15 秒，多則 30 秒，只花幾秒的時間用一個句子回答問題，後面就是一片空白，會讓你的回答聽起來非常沒有誠意，分數也不會高。而且在這部分的一開始也提到「請在作答時間內儘量的表達」，所以答題時不是「回答問題就好」，而是要「多說一點」。

2. 閱卷老師並不會去調查你是不是誠實回答，所以很多回答可以根據你會的詞彙、表達方式，所以當場編造也沒關係。例如假設週末要去逛故宮，但你對逛故宮會用到的英文單字不熟，也沒有把握，就不要乖乖的講故宮之

旅，捏造一個「全家出遊」的計畫也可以。

Well, I don't really have anything planned for the coming weekend. I think I will just stay home and play my favorite computer game. Unless it is a family day, I prefer to stay home because many places are usually crowded on the weekend.

嗯，針對即將到來的週末假期，我真的沒有什麼計畫。我想我只會待在家裡玩我最喜歡的電腦遊戲。除非那天是家庭日，否則我比較喜歡待在家裡，因為週末許多地方通常都是人擠人。

My family and I are going to a holiday resort in Hualien. We will be going there by car, so we can enjoy the scenery better. I missed the clear blue sea in Hualien. We will be staying at a hotel located in the mountains, and I hope to see many stars in the sky.

我和家人要去花蓮的度假勝地。我們會開車過去，這樣就更可以好好地享受風景。我很想念花蓮清澈的藍色海洋。我們會待在位於山中的飯店，而且我希望能看到許多天空中的星星。

重點補充

以下是週末可能會做的活動：

go shopping 購物、see a movie 看電影、meet some friends 跟朋友見面、dating my boyfriend/girlfriend 跟男 / 女朋友約會、go to some bookstores 逛書店。

2 What is your favorite color? Why? What's so special about it?

你最喜歡的顏色是什麼？為什麼？它有什麼特別之處？

答題策略

1. 本題一定要知道 favorite 是「最喜歡的」的意思才能作答。喜歡的原因除了針對顏色本身給人的一般印象外，也可以用該顏色對你有何特別意義（像是和你某個收藏品的顏色一樣等）來著墨。
2. 開頭除了重複 My favorite color is... 外，也可以使用 I like... the most，使用不一樣的單字、句型來換句話說。

回答範例 1

My favorite color is blue. Blue is the color of the sea and the sky. I think blue is also a nice color for clothes. Most jeans are blue, and I have a pair of blue sneakers. I don't understand why people say Monday blues. To me, blue is not a sad color.

我最喜歡的顏色是藍色。藍色是海及天空的顏色。我覺得就服裝來説，藍色也是很好的顏色。大部分的牛仔褲是藍色的，而且我有一雙藍色的運動鞋。我不懂為什麼人們説「星期一是 blue（憂鬱）的」。對我來説，藍色不是悲傷的顏色。

回答範例 2

White is my favorite color because it goes well with any other color. I can match white with pink, blue or yellow. I think white is a special color because it is pure. That is why wedding gowns are usually white. The only bad thing about white is that it gets dirty easily.

白色是我最喜歡的顏色，因為它跟其他任何顏色都很搭。我可以用粉紅色、藍色或黃色來搭配白色。我認為白色是一個特別的顏色，因為它很純淨。這也是為什麼婚紗通常是白色的。白色唯一不好的地方就是很容易弄髒。

重點補充

針對題目所問的問題，有時候會出現真的不知道要説什麼，或者沒有特別的看法的情形。不過總不能説我沒有最喜歡的顏色，然後什麼都不説，這樣的話就只能期待重考了。遇到這種情形，可先用 Well, it depends.（嗯，要看情況），然後再間接回答問題。例如：

27

Well, it depends. I don't have any favorite color. Different colors look good on different things. I always wear blue jeans, but if I want to buy a car, I don't think I will buy a blue car. I will probably choose black because it looks pretty cool, and it doesn't get dirty as easily as a white car.

嗯，要看情況。我沒有最喜歡的顏色。不同顏色在不同的事物上都會有好看之處。我總是穿藍色牛仔褲，但是如果我要買車子，我不認為我會買藍色的車子。我應該會選擇黑色，因為黑色看起來挺酷的，而且不像白色的一樣容易弄髒。

3 What is your least favorite subject in school? What difficulties do you face?

你在學校最不喜歡的科目是什麼？你碰到了什麼樣的困難？

答題策略

1. 雖然這是口說測驗，但聽力還是很重要的，如果只聽到 favorite 就開始作答，內容就會答非所問。least favorite 意思是「最不喜歡的」，如同 least expensive 意思是「最不貴的」。在回答問題的部分，一個題目通常會有第二個問句，主要是給考生一點提示，讓考生有更多東西可以講。

2. 可直接詳答 My least favorite subject in school is...（我在學校最不喜歡的科目是…），當然也可以直接說出最不喜歡的科目，不過也可換個方式來說，有助於加強表達能力，例如：I think it must be...（我想一定是…）。

回答範例 1

My least favorite subject is math. I used to like math in elementary school but it got really confusing since junior high school. I find the concepts too hard to understand, and no matter how hard I tried, I couldn't pass the math exams.

我最不喜歡的科目是數學。在國小的時候我曾經喜歡數學，但是自從上了國中，數學變得很難理解。我發現那些概念太難理解，而且不管我多麼努力，我就是無法通過數學測驗。

回答範例 2

History is my worst subject in school now. I enjoy reading the stories but I hate to memorize names, dates and places. I don't understand why students are tested on such minor details. Studying for history tests is really time-consuming.

歷史是我現在最差的科目。我喜歡閱讀那些故事,但是我很討厭背名字、日期和地點。我不明白為什麼學生要考這種小細節。為歷史測驗做考前準備是非常耗時的一件事。

重點補充

由於現在是考英文,如果回答自己最不喜歡的科目是英文,好像有點怪怪的。不過只要說得出具體的理由來,還是可以被接受。

Though I am taking this English exam, English is my least favorite subject in school. I mean I like English when I use to talk with people but I hate it when I have to remember many grammar rules. The way my school teacher teaches English is really boring.

雖然我正在考這場英文測驗,英文卻是我在學校最不喜歡的科目。我的意思是,當我用英文跟別人交談時,我很喜歡英文,但是必須記很多文法規則的時候,我就很討厭英文。我的學校老師教英文的方式真的很無聊。

4 Do you have a cellphone? What do you usually use it for?

你有手機嗎?你通常用手機來做什麼?

答題策略

1. 有時候題目太簡單,反而不好發揮。現在這個年代,多數人都有手機。手機除了打電話,就是玩遊戲、傳 LINE 和在 Facebook(臉書)上貼照片。可以簡單把這些事情串成句子,就能充分回答這個題目。

2. 不是所有人都有可上網的智慧型手機,如果你拿的是傳統手機,除了打電話以外,手機也可以當字典和鬧鐘。不喜歡用手機玩遊戲的話也可以提出來,說這麼做很浪費時間。

Yes, I have a smartphone, and besides making calls, I usually use it to surf the Net. I downloaded a few games, and now I use my cellphone to play them. I also use my cellphone to access Instagram and post photos on it. I also use an application called LINE to send messages to my friends.

有的，我有智慧型手機，除了打電話以外，我通常用它來上網。我之前下載了一些遊戲，現在我用手機來玩這些遊戲。我還用手機上 Instagram，並在上面發佈照片。我也用一個叫做 LINE 的應用程式來傳訊息給我的朋友。

I have a cellphone but I can use it to surf the Net only in places with free Wi-Fi service. There is a dictionary function in it, so I use it to help myself learn English. I also use my cellphone as an alarm clock. I don't use my cellphone to play games because it is a waste of time.

我有手機，但我只能在有免費 Wi-Fi 服務的地方上網。我的手機裡有字典的功能，所以我用它來幫助我學英文。我也用手機當做鬧鐘。我不用手機玩遊戲，因為這樣做是浪費時間。

重點補充

如果是沒有手機的人怎麼辦？難道說我沒有手機就結束？當然不行，沒有手機也可以利用 Who，What，When，Where，Why 等提問幫助你說出一些內容。

No, I don't have a cellphone. (Who?) My mom says I am too young to have a cellphone. (Why?) She says it will affect my schoolwork. (When?) I think she will buy a smartphone for me only when I enter senior high school. Honestly, I don't mind living without a cellphone.

不，我沒有手機。我媽媽說我太小了不能有手機。她說手機會影響我的學業。我認為只有在我念高中時她才會買手機給我。老實說，我不介意過沒有手機的日子。

第 1 回

第 2 回

第 3 回

第 4 回

第 5 回

第 6 回

5 Have you ever considered becoming a police officer? What do you feel about being a police officer in Taiwan?

你曾經考慮過要當警察嗎？你對於在台灣當警察有什麼看法？

答題策略

1. 從關鍵詞 police officer（警官）可理解這題問的是你有沒有想過要當警察。回答「是」的話可以陳述當警察的好處，回答「不」的話則可以談到不適合當警察的原因。

2. 如果還沒拿定主意，也可以談一下當警察的優缺點，接著說自己還在考慮當中。

回答範例 1

I have never thought about it. I don't think I want to be a police officer as it can be a dangerous job. Besides, a policeman has to work irregular hours. I think it is hard to be a police officer in Taiwan because many people do not respect the law.

我從來沒想過這件事。我不想要當警察，因為這是份危險的工作。此外，警察的工作時間不規律。我認為在台灣當警察很困難，因為許多人不尊重法律。

回答範例 2

That idea has crossed my mind before. My parents keep telling me how great it is to be a police officer. They think it is a stable job with high pay and good benefits. Personally, I am a little tempted but I think I still have a few years to think about my career options.

我之前曾經有那個想法。我的父母一直告訴我當警察有多好。他們認為這是一份穩定的工作，而且有高薪和很好的福利。就個人而言，我有一點心動，但是我想我還有好幾年的時間來思考我的職業選擇。

萬一題目問的行業自己完全沒想過,一時之間反應不過來的話,還有一招救命法寶,就是把話題帶到別的地方去。

I'm not sure. I have not thought about it yet. I have wanted to be an artist since I was young. I love to draw pictures, and I hope I can find a job that I am interested in. Maybe I can be an art teacher at school. That will be great.

我不確定。我還沒有想過這件事。我從小就想當藝術家。我喜歡畫圖,所以我希望可以找到一份我有興趣的工作。或許我可以成為學校的美術老師。那樣就太好了。

6 Talk about a book you have read or a movie you have watched before. Who are the characters? How will you rate the book or the movie?

談談某一本你讀過的書或某一部你看過的電影。那些角色是誰?你會如何評價這本書或電影?

答題策略

1. 許多考生遇到的難題是,題目聽得懂但是不知道要說什麼。建議預先想好自己喜歡的書或電影,到時候才能對答如流。
2. 書籍包括 novel(小說)或 self-help book(自助書)等。電影分為 action movie(動作片)、thriller(驚悚片)、science fiction film(科幻)、romance(愛情)、comedy(喜劇)等。

回答範例 1

I read a novel called *The Hunger Games* recently. It is about a teenage girl who fought to stay alive. The main character in the story is brave and compassionate. I will give this a nine out of ten, and I recommend all teenagers to read it. There are three books in the series but I think the first one is the best. I did not really enjoy the other two. By the way, all the books have been adapted and made into movies.

我最近讀了一本叫《飢餓遊戲》的小說。這是關於一名少女為了生存而奮鬥的故事。故事裡的主角很勇敢也很有同情心。滿分十分我會給這本書打九分，並推薦所有青少年看這本書。這個系列一共有三本書，但是我認為第一本是最棒的。我不是很喜歡閱讀另外兩集。順便一提，全部的書已經被改編、製作成電影。

回答範例 2

I seldom go to the theater but I watched a movie on the Internet not long ago. It was a science fiction movie about aliens from other planets. Frankly speaking, I have no idea what the message behind the movie was. I guess it is just another movie about aliens. I can't even recall the name of the movie. Anyway, I watched it for free so I shouldn't be complaining about it. I think a good movie is one that makes you think about some issues in life after watching it.

我很少去電影院，但是不久前我在網路上看過一部電影。那一部科幻片是關於來自其他星球的外星人。坦白說，我不知道這部電影背後想要傳達什麼訊息。我想這只是另外一部關於外星人的電影。我甚至連片名也想不起來。不管怎樣，我是看免費的，所以我不應該抱怨什麼。我認為一部好的電影，會讓你在看完之後去思考人生中的一些議題。

重點補充

如果看的是中文電影，可能無法馬上知道該電影的名稱要怎麼翻譯成英文，主要人物的英文名字也只能用音譯的方式。即使是這樣，還是可以簡單說明劇情，並提到自己喜不喜歡這部電影，以及為什麼喜歡。

I watched a movie recently but I don't know the name of the movie in English. It's about a man and a woman falling in love. It's really funny, and I enjoyed watching it. The man is a famous actor, and he is very handsome, but I don't remember his real name.

我最近看了一部電影，但是我不知道這部電影的英文名稱。那是關於一個男人和一個女人相戀的劇情。內容真的很好笑，我看得很開心。那位男的是一位知名演員，而且他很帥，但我不記得他的真實姓名。

Who influenced you the most in your life? In what ways did the person change you?

誰對你的人生影響最大？這個人在什麼方面改變了你？

答題策略

1. 這題有一點難度，若無事先準備，可能會說不到一句話就結束了。回答這類有深度的問題，有兩種方法：一種是一般的回答方式，用許多人會想到的方式回答。例如，影響我最深的人當然是我偉大的母親。
2. 第二種方式是讓人意想不到的回答。例如，影響我最深的人是某位歷史人物或名人。

回答範例 1

The person who influenced me the most is my mother. She is always there for me, and she talks with me like a friend. She doesn't force me to agree with her but gives me sound advice when I need it. One thing she always says is to be responsible for your own decisions and behavior. We often talk about the value of life and how to be a better person. I have many weaknesses, and my mom helps me to turn them into strengths. My mom understands that no one is perfect and we have to learn to live with that.

影響我最大的人是我的母親。她總是支持我，而且跟我說話時就像朋友一樣。她不強迫我認同她的意見，但是當我需要的時候，她會給我完善的建議。她總是說的一句話是，要為你自己的決定和行為負責。我們常常談論生命的價值，以及如何成為一個更好的人。我有許多弱點，而我的母親幫助我把這些弱點轉變成優點。我媽媽了解沒有人是完美的，我們必須學習接受這一點。

回答範例 2

You may not believe it, but the person who influenced me the most is Steve Jobs. I read his biography, and I also watched a speech he gave to some university graduates on YouTube. Though he is no

第 1 回

第 2 回
第 3 回
第 4 回
第 5 回
第 6 回

longer with us, his story inspired me. Steve Jobs talked about how important it is to love the work you do and to find out what you truly love. He was a billionaire but he didn't really care about the money. He wanted to make a difference to the world and contribute to mankind.

你或許不相信，但是影響我最深的人是賈伯斯。我讀了他的傳記，我也在 YouTube 上看了他給一些大學畢業生的演講。雖然他已不在我們身邊，他的故事還是給了我啟發。賈伯斯談到去愛自己的工作，以及找出自己真正喜歡做的事情有多麼重要。他是億萬富翁，但是他卻不在乎錢。他想要做的是讓自己對世界有所改變，並對人類做出貢獻。

重點補充

如果你想不出誰對你的影響最大。如果要據實回答，可以說，在人生的不同階段有不同的人影響你。

Well, this is a tough question. I can't think of anyone right now. Different people influenced me in different ways and at different stages in my life. I used to hate English. I remembered a teacher who helped me. He made English really interesting. Because of that, I started to like English.

嗯，這是個困難的問題。我現在想不到任何人。不同的人在我生命中的不同階段，以不同的方式影響我。我曾經很討厭英文。我記得有一位老師幫助過我。他讓英文變得很有趣。因為如此，我開始喜歡英文。

8 Have you ever bought anything on the Internet? Why or why not?

你曾經在網路上買過任何東西嗎？為什麼買？為什麼沒有買？

答題策略

1. 這題相對來說簡單一點，如果有在網路上買過東西就說「有」，然後舉例說明，再談一談網路購物的好處，例如「比較便宜」，「很方便」等。
2. 若回答說不喜歡在網路上買東西，也必須說明原因。像是可能曾經受騙等理由，再順便提出網路購物的壞處。

I bought a T-shirt on the Internet once, and I told myself I will never buy clothes on the Internet again. The T-shirt is made of bad material, and it shrunk after I washed it. I bought it because it looked nice and was cheaper compared to the same brand sold in department stores. I guess I was fooled by the picture and the lower price. There are certain things that you shouldn't buy on the Internet, and in my personal experience, clothes are one of them.

有一次我在網路上買了一件 T 恤，接著我告訴自己，以後絕不會在網路上買衣服了。那件 T 恤的質料很差，而且在我洗了之後就縮水了。我買那件衣服是因為它很好看，而且也比在百貨公司賣的同樣品牌便宜。我猜我被照片和比較低的價格騙了。有些東西就是不應該在網路上買的，以我個人的經驗而言，衣服就是其中之一。

Yes. I love online shopping. You can get things at a discount and you don't even have to leave your house. It's so convenient. I bought many things on the Net, including a watch, some computer games, novels and even sandwiches. However, I pay for the items I have ordered only when they are delivered to me. I read about cases where people were cheated of their money when they used their credit cards to pay.

是的。我喜愛網路購物。你可以用折扣價買東西，而且你甚至不用離開家門。真是方便。我在網路上買了很多東西，包括手錶、一些電腦遊戲、小說，甚至是三明治。然而，我只使用貨到付款。我讀過一些人們用信用卡付款後被騙了的案例。

重點補充

假設你因為家裡沒有網路，或者從來沒有上網購物過，還是說比較喜歡到實體店面買東西的情況時，請參考以下的敘述。

I have never bought anything online. I know it is more convenient, but I prefer to shop in department stores. I can see and touch the things before deciding if I want to buy them. I think it is better this way, especially for things like clothes and food. I guess I am a little old-fashioned.

我從來沒有在網路上買過任何東西。我知道網路購物是比較方便，但是我比較喜歡在百貨公司裡購物。在決定購買之前，我可以看到並碰觸到那些東西。我認為這樣比較好，特別是像衣服和食物之類的東西。我想我可能有點老派。

9 Why do you think night markets are so popular in Taiwan?

你認為為什麼夜市在台灣這麼受歡迎？

答題策略

1. 30 秒的時間不算短，如果隨便交代幾句可能 10 秒內就說完了，留下 20 秒的空白恐怕很難過關。建議把這些 30 秒的題目當成寫作文的題目，內容分為開頭，舉例說明和結尾。開頭可先提到 Night markets represent a unique culture of Taiwan.（夜市代表台灣的一種獨一無二的文化），或者 The night market is a part of Taiwanese culture.（夜市是台灣文化的一部分）。

2. 若想不出漂亮的字句，可以簡單敘述自己去夜市的原因和經驗，並說明大人、小孩都喜歡夜市的原因。

回答範例 1

Night markets represent a unique culture of Taiwan. The main attraction of night markets is the wide variety of food available. Eating stinky tofu and oyster omelets at night markets is a special experience. What's more, the food sold at night markets is much cheaper compared to restaurants. Besides food, night markets also sell clothing, accessories, toys and so on. Not to forget the different kinds of games that both kids and adults find interesting.

夜市代表了台灣的一種獨一無二的文化。夜市主要吸引人的地方是可以買到各式各樣的美食。在夜市吃臭豆腐和蚵仔煎是一種特別的體驗。而且，在夜市販賣的食物比起餐廳便宜許多。除了食物之外，夜市也賣衣物、飾品、玩具等等。也別忘了大人、小孩都覺得有趣的各種遊戲。

I go to the night market near my home at least once a month. Personally, I enjoy the food as well as the atmosphere. I think it is a fun place for families and friends to visit. Kids love the night market because they can play many games and win prizes. Adults can do some shopping, and very often people can find good bargains at a night market. I have been to night markets since I was a child. I think night markets in Taiwan have a special place in my heart.

我一個月至少會去一次我家附近的夜市。以我個人來說，我喜歡那裡的食物還有氣氛。我認為夜市是個有趣的地方，適合家人和朋友去。小朋友喜歡夜市，因為他們可以玩很多遊戲並贏得獎品。大人可以去購物，而且常常在夜市可以找到物美價廉的東西。我從小的時候就去過夜市了。我認為台灣的夜市在我心中有一個特別的地位。

重點補充

你也可以提出反面的意見，說你不喜歡去夜市，不過題目問的是「夜市為什麼這麼受歡迎」，所以你還是必須提到夜市受歡迎的原因。

I seldom visit the night market. It is always crowded with people. There are many Chinese tourists at some famous night markets. I think night markets are popular because the food is cheap and delicious. The clothes and other things sold in night markets are also less expensive.

我很少去夜市。那裡總是擠滿人。在一些著名的夜市裡有很多中國遊客。我認為夜市受歡迎是因為食物便宜又好吃。在夜市販售的衣服和其他東西也比較不貴。

10 How do you maintain a healthy lifestyle? How do you keep yourself healthy?

你如何維持健康的生活方式呢？你如何讓自己保持健康呢？

答題策略

1. 要維持健康的生活方式，不外乎是 a balanced diet（飲食均衡）、regular exercise（規律運動）、enough sleep（睡眠充足），還有保持 cheerful and positive（愉快、正面的心情），這些表達都可以用在回答裡。

回答範例 1

First, I keep my weight under control by having a balanced diet. I avoid eating fast food and other oily food. Second, I exercise on a regular basis. I go jogging twice a week, and sometimes I play badminton with my friends. Third, I go to bed before 11 p.m. and make sure I have enough sleep. Finally, I remind myself to be cheerful and positive. It's unhealthy if I am angry with someone or worried about something.

首先，我藉由均衡的飲食來控制體重。我不吃速食和其他油膩的食物。第二，我規律運動。我一個星期去慢跑兩次，有時候也跟我的朋友打羽球。第三，我在晚上十一點之前就去睡覺，並確保我有充足的睡眠。最後，我提醒自己要開心和樂觀。如果我生別人的氣或擔心某件事的話是不健康的。

重點補充

以上回答的要點應該在考試前準備好，如果沒有的話，只好想到什麼說什麼，用自己的親身經歷做為內容。

Health is very important. I live a healthy life because I play basketball with my friends at least twice a week. I drink a lot of water. My mom always reminds me of that. I also eat a lot of vegetables and fruits. I go to bed early and sleep about eight to nine hours every day. One more thing, I don't smoke.

健康是很重要的。我過著健康的生活，因為我和朋友每週至少打籃球兩次。我喝很多水，我媽媽總是提醒我這一點，我也吃很多蔬菜和水果。我很早上床睡覺，而且每天大概睡八到九個小時。還有一件事，我不抽菸。

▶▶▶ 第三部分 **看圖敘述**

下面有一張圖片及四個相關的問題,請在 1 分半鐘內完成作答。作答時,請直接回答,不需將題號及題目唸出。

首先請利用 30 秒的時間看圖及問題。

 1. 照片裡的人在什麼地方?
2. 照片裡的人在做什麼?
3. 照片裡的人為什麼會在那裡?
4. 如果尚有時間,請詳細描述圖片中的景物。

草稿擬定

1. 照片裡的人在什麼地方?夜市 night market、戶外 outdoor
2. 照片裡的人在做什麼?販賣餐點 selling meals、等候餐點 waiting for order
3. 照片裡的人為什麼在這裡?外帶餐點 food takeout
4. 如果尚有時間,請詳細描述圖中的景物。沒有內用的桌椅 no tables or chairs for people to finish their food、空杯子 spare cups、醬料 sauce

第 1 回

第 2 回
第 3 回
第 4 回
第 5 回
第 6 回

高分 SOP

看圖敘述的祕訣是，不要一次把看到的東西說完，否則很難講到一分半鐘。每張圖的表達流程，不外乎是 Who，What，When，Where，Why 等問句。建議從 Where 開始，先說這張圖應該是在哪裡拍攝的，並舉出圖中的背景或其他事物加以證明。接著就是 Who，圖中若只有一或兩個人物，可針對人物的外貌和年齡簡單帶過。若人物眾多，可挑出一兩個重要人物，說明他們的身分是什麼，他們在做什麼（what），若人物的表情看得清楚的話也可以加以敘述。然後針對人物的動作或表情再提出 Why，為什麼他們要這麼做，你認為其中的原因是什麼。至於時間（When）可以說一說照片拍攝的時間點可能是什麼時候，所以圖中人物才會做這些事情。如果還有時間的話，可以針對 How，提出你個人的看法和觀察。

以照片中夜市的攤位為例，如果說：「這是一個賣輕食、飲料的攤位，有幾個人在排隊，也有幾個店員在準備食物。」，這樣可能不到 10 秒就說完了，後面也很難再接下去。因此，請用上面提到的表達流程，來組織要講的內容，同時也參考以下的萬用句來強化、修飾自己的表達。

必殺萬用句

1. I am not mistaken, this picture was taken in a...（如果我沒有弄錯的話，這張照片是在…拍攝的）
   這是可以套用在任何一個看圖敘述題的句型，直接說明我們對拍攝地點的判斷。因為常會有一些照片是沒有拍到全景的，可能會判斷錯誤，所以特地用一句「如果我沒有弄錯的話」，即使說錯了，和圖片的狀況不太一樣，考官還是會覺得這個考生的表達技巧不錯。

2. There are also some / many / a lot of... in the picture. 中，要切記「圖中有…」的「有」必須用 There，並且在後面再加 be 動詞，不能說 There have，否則這個文法錯誤是會扣分的。

3. I see... in the background. 這個句型用來佐證我們對於地點的推斷。例如先說「這是 night market（夜市）」，然後再用 I see a restaurant in the background. 來支持我們前面提到的「夜市」的說法，這種方式除了在本題，也可以同時運用在其他各種看圖敘述題。

4. 針對人物或事物的敘述，很確定的話可以用 it is obvious that...（很明顯的是），不是很確定的話，可以説 might be（也許是）或 could be（可能是）。

5. 若是要補充説明，可以用 What's more 來表示。

回答範例

If I am not mistaken, this picture was taken at a night market. There are quite a few people in the picture. I see a restaurant in the background. Judging from the picture, I think the store might be selling light meals or beverages like juice and milk tea. The people in the picture are standing in front of the counter, waiting for their order. Like in the picture, more and more people in Taiwan choose food takeout or food delivery, especially during the epidemic period at present. Therefore, it is obvious that there are not any tables or chairs for them to finish their food at the store. What's more, I can see that the spare cups and the sauce are available for those to help themselves as the customers prefer to have meals to go. If the picture was taken nowadays in Taiwan, I would say it tells something happening here when we are out for food.

範例中譯

如果我沒弄錯的話，這張照片是在夜市拍的。照片裡有幾個人，我看到背景有一間餐廳。從照片上來看，我認為這家店可能在賣輕食或是果汁及奶茶等飲料。照片裡的人站在櫃台前，等候他們點的餐；就像照片所看到的，台灣越來越多人選擇外帶或外送，尤其在目前疫情期間更是如此，因此，很明顯可以看出店家不提供桌椅作為內用。還有，因為顧客偏好餐點外帶，我可以看到有提供空杯及醬料讓他們自取。如果這張照片是在台灣拍的話，我會說它有透露出目前我們外出覓食的現況。

第二回 寫作能力測驗答題注意事項

1. 本測驗共有兩部分。第一部分為中譯英,第二部分為英文作文。測驗時間為 **40 分鐘**。

2. 請利用試題紙空白處背面擬稿,但正答務必書寫在「寫作能力測驗答案紙」上。在答案紙以外的地方作答,不予計分。

3. 第一部分中譯英請在答案紙第一頁作答,第二部分英文作文請在答案紙第二頁作答。

4. 作答時請勿隔行書寫,請注意字跡清晰可讀,並保持答案紙之清潔,以免影響評分。

5. 測驗時,不得在准考證或其他物品上抄題,亦不得有傳遞、夾帶小抄、左顧右盼或交談等違規行為。

6. 意圖或已經將試題紙攜出試場者,五年內不得報名參加本測驗。請人代考者,連同代考者,三年內不得報名參加本測驗。

7. 測驗結束時,須立即停止作答,在原位靜候監試人員收回全部試題紙及答案紙,清點無誤後,宣佈結束始可離場。

8. 應試者入場、出場及測驗中如有違反上列規則或不服監試人員之指示者,監試人員得取消應試資格並請其離場,且作答不予計分。

全民英語能力分級檢定測驗

中級寫作能力測驗

本測驗共有兩部份。第一部份為中譯英，第二部份為英文寫作。測驗時間為 40 分鐘。

一、中譯英 (40%)

說明：請將下列的一段中文翻譯成通順、達意且前後連貫的英文。

> 山姆(Sam)還有一個月就要從高中畢業了。儘管他的朋友都忙著申請大學，他卻有別的計畫。山姆打算先到國外打工。一則，他可以獲得寶貴的工作經驗。二則，他可以存一筆錢。最棒的是，他可以在休假時在那個國家旅遊。

二、英文作文 (60%)

請依下面所提供的文字提示寫一篇英文作文，長度約 120 字（8 至 12 個句子）。作文可以是一個完整的段落，也可以分段。（評分重點包括內容、組織、文法、用字遣詞、標點符號、大小寫。）

提示：不管是在平板電腦或手機，網路遊戲都大受歡迎。有人覺得這些遊戲對學業和健康方面會產生負面影響，也有人認為這些遊戲只不過是一種消遣，有助於紓解壓力也可以打發時間。請提出你自己的看法。

全民英語能力分級檢定測驗中級寫作能力答案紙

第一部份請由第 1 行開始作答，請勿隔行書寫。

5

10

15

20

25

30

35

40

第二回　口說能力測驗答題注意事項

1. 本測驗問題由耳機播放，回答則經麥克風錄下。分朗讀短文、回答問題與看圖敘述三部分，時間共約 15 分鐘，連同口試說明時間共需約五十分鐘。

2. 第一部份朗讀短文有 1 分鐘準備時間，此時請勿唸出聲音，待聽到「請開始朗讀」2 分鐘的朗讀時間開始時，再將短文唸出來。第二部分回答問題的題目將播出 2 遍，聽完第二次題目後要立即回答。第三部份看圖敘述有 30 秒的思考時間及 1 分 30 秒的答題時間，思考時不可在試題紙上作記號，亦不可出聲。等聽到指示開始回答時，請您針對圖片盡量的回答。

3. 錄音設備皆已事先完成設定，請勿觸動任何機件，以免影響錄音。測驗時請戴妥耳機，將麥克風調到嘴邊約三公分處，聽清楚說明，依指示以適中音量回答。

4. 評分人員將根據您錄下的回答（發音與語調、語法與字彙、可解度及切題度等）作整體的評分。您可利用所附光碟自行測試，一一錄下回答後，再播出來聽聽，並斟酌調整。練習時請盡量以英語思考、應對，考試時較易有自然的表現。

5. 請注意測試時不可在試題紙上劃線、打「√」或作任何記號；不可在准考證或其他物品上抄題；亦不可有傳遞、夾帶小抄、左顧右盼或交談等違規行為。

6. 意圖或已將試題紙或試題影音資料攜出或傳送出試場者，視同侵犯本中心著作財產權，限五年內不得報名參加「全民英檢」測驗。請人代考，連同代考者，三年內不得報名參加本測驗。

7. 測驗結束時，須立即停止作答，在原位靜候監試人員收回全部試題紙且清點無誤後，等候監試人員宣布結束後始可離場。

8. 入場、出場及測驗中如有違反規則或不服監試人員指示者，監試人員將取消您的應試資格並請您離場，且作答不予計分，亦不退費。

全民英語能力分級檢定測驗

中級口說能力測驗

請在 15 秒內完成並唸出下列自我介紹的句子：

My seat number is（座位號碼後 5 碼）, and my registration number is
（考試號碼後 5 碼）.

第一部分：朗讀短文

　　請先利用一分鐘的時間閱讀下面的短文，然後在二分鐘內以正常的速度，清楚正確的讀出下面的短文。

　　A majority of Hollywood blockbuster movies have certain elements in common: romance, fantasy, thrills and comedy. Themes that bring tears to our eyes seem to be the minority. Nowadays, the audience prefers laughter to sadness. Another interesting trend is the rise of horror movies. The more frightened viewers are, the more they love it.

　　　　　　　　*　　　　　　　　　　*　　　　　　　　　　*

　　Despite the fact that music is not one of my strengths, I still enjoy listening to songs. I can't play any musical instrument, yet I can indulge myself in graceful melodies. I know nothing about classical music, but I have a special liking for pop music. Except heavy rock, I love all kinds of music. As a writer, music is my main source of inspiration.

第二部分：回答問題

　　這個部分共有 10 題。題目已事先錄音，每題經由耳機播出二次，不印在試卷上。第一至五題，每題回答時間 15 秒；第六至十題，每題回答時間 30 秒。每題播出後，請立即回答。回答時，不一定要用完整的句子，但請在作答時間內儘量的表達。

第三部分：看圖敘述

　　下面有一張圖片及四個相關的問題，請在一分半鐘內完成作答。作答時，請直接回答，不需將題號及題目唸出。

　　首先請利用 30 秒的時間看圖及問題。

提示：
1. 照片裡的人在什麼地方？
2. 照片裡的人在做什麼？
3. 照片裡的人為什麼會在那裡？
4. 如果尚有時間，請詳細描述圖片中的景物。

請將下列自我介紹的句子再唸一遍：

My seat number is（座位號碼後 5 碼）, and my registration number is （考試號碼後 5 碼）.

複試 寫作測驗 解析

▶▶▶ 第一部分 **中譯英** (40%)

請將下列的一段中文翻譯成通順、達意且前後連貫的英文。

山姆還有一個月就要從高中畢業了。儘管他的朋友都忙著申請大學,他卻有別的計畫。山姆打算先到國外打工。一則,他可以獲得寶貴的工作經驗。二則,他可以存一筆錢。最棒的是,他可以在休假時在那個國家旅遊。

翻譯範例

Sam will be graduating from senior high school in another month's time. Although his friends are busy applying for universities, he has other plans. Sam intends to work overseas first. For one, he can gain valuable job experience. For another, he can save up a sum of money. The best part is, he can travel in that country during his off-days.

逐句說明

1. 山姆還有一個月就要從高中畢業了。

Sam will be graduating from senior high school in another month's time.

從「還有一個月就要…畢業了」可知,目前他還沒畢業,因此時態要用未來式。範例答案的 will be graduating 用的是未來進行式。其實,用未來簡單式 will graduate 也可以,只不過文中強調「未來的某個時間點某人將會做什麼」,因此用未來進行式比較貼切,就像 Richard Max 的不朽名曲 Right Here Waiting 中的歌詞:Wherever you go, whatever you do, I will be right here waiting for you.。從某學校畢業,介系詞用 from。介系詞 in 後面加上一段時間,表示「在…之後」。例如,I will be back in an hour 表示「我一個小時之後會回來」。

2. 儘管他的朋友都忙著申請大學，他卻有別的計畫。

Although his friends are busy applying for universities, he has other plans.

　　英文的邏輯不同於中文，連接詞的功能是連接兩個句子，兩個句子由一個連接詞串連起來，因此不能用到兩個連接詞。這就是為什麼英文「有 although（雖然）就沒 but（但是）」，「有 because（因為）就沒 so（所以）」的原因。「忙著」表示某個動作還在進行中，因此時態要用進行式，S + be + busy + V-ing。「忙著申請大學」要用現在進行式 are busy applying for universities。apply（申請…），介系詞用 for。

　　當「計畫」是指某種想法時，通常用複數的 plans。other 在這裡有形容詞的功能，修飾 plans，表示「其他的」。others 是指「其他人」或「其他事物」，為代名詞功能，而且是複數形。「其他的學生呢？」可說 Where are the other students?「其他人（或東西）呢？」可說 Where are the others?

3. 山姆打算先到國外打工。

Sam intends to work overseas first.

　　打算（intend）和想要（want）、計畫（plan）的意思差不多，但是 intend 屬於高中的單字，正確運用 intend 會有加分效果。切記主詞 Sam 為第三人稱單數，因此動詞必須用單數，也就是動詞字尾有加上 s。這個規則從國小就教過了，可是因為中文沒有這樣的概念，因此很多人會疏忽。可把主詞、動詞一致原則簡單地理解為：因為是 He is 所以要用 He intends，字尾都是 s。overseas 和 abroad 都是「國外」的意思。到國外念書為 study overseas 或 study abroad。英翻中的其中一個挑戰是，不能從中文的字面意義直接翻譯成英文，中文我們會說：「他打算先到國外打工」，英文的 first（先）是副詞，通常用在句尾，例如，He went home first.（他先回家）。

4. 一則，他可以獲得寶貴的工作經驗。二則，他可以存一筆錢。

For one, he can gain valuable job experience. For another, he can save up a sum of money.

　　陳述論點時常用「First 首先」，「Second 其次」，「Last 最後」，因為前面已經用了副詞 first，不想重複使用而影響表達能力，因此選擇用「For one 一則」，「For another 二則；其次」，下一句再接「The best part is 最棒的是」。

　　「獲得」也可以用 get 或 have，但是 experience（經驗）通常和 gain（取得）搭配，是比較好的表達方式。有一句英文俚語是 No Pain, No Gain，沒有疼痛就沒有收穫，意思是「不付出就不會有收穫」。

　　「寶貴的工作經驗」的表達中，用 valuable 比 precious（珍貴）更適合，因為 precious 比較適合用在形容稀少或難得的事物。

　　save 加上介系詞 up 有「存錢」和「儲蓄」的意思，單純動詞 save 則是「省錢」的意思。假設某件原價一千元的物品「打了八折，可以省下兩百元」，英文可說 It's 20% off. You can save NT $200.。這個片語可以用一句英文俚語來記，Save up for rainy days，意思是「未雨綢繆」。

　　a sum of money（一筆錢）。本題的「一筆錢」也可翻譯成 some money（一些錢），只不過這樣無法展現英檢中級程度該有的表達能力。sum 和 total 都有「總數」的意思，是表達錢的量詞。金額相當大時可以說：「It's not a small sum of money（這不是一筆小錢）」。

5. 最棒的是，他可以在休假時在那個國家旅遊。

The best part is, he can travel in that country during his off-days.

　　嚴格來說，這句應該由 that 引導的名詞子句連接，變成 The best part is that he can travel in that country during his off-days。然而用逗點也可以接受，因為在說話時，說到 The best part is，通常會稍微停頓再描述下面的事項。「值勤中」是 on duty，「沒有在值勤」是 off-duty，off-day 是「放假日」，但是「今天要上班」不能說 on day，要說 Today is my workday. I have to work today。「明天要請假」可以說 May I take a day off tomorrow?。還有，若是要到國外工作的話，應該要先問清楚「一個月休幾天」，How many off-days do I have a month?

▶▶▶ 第二部分 英文作文 (60%)

　　請依下面所提供的文字提示寫一篇英文作文，長度約 120 字（8 至 12 個句子）。作文可以是一個完整的段落，也可以分段。

提示 不管是在平板電腦或手機，網路遊戲都大受歡迎。有人覺得網路遊戲對

學業和健康方面會產生負面影響，也有人認為這些遊戲只不過是一種消遣，有助於紓解壓力也可以打發時間。請提出你自己的看法。

結構預設

本題主要是請你說明使用平板電腦或手機玩網路遊戲的利與弊。若立場中立，可提出使用平板電腦或手機的好處和壞處。在最後一句做總結時，給使用平板電腦和手機的人一些建議。

草稿擬定

1. 利與弊 pros and cons
2. 好處：娛樂與消遣 entertainment and recreation，紓解壓力 relieve stress。
3. 壞處：負面影響 harmful effects，上癮 addicted to，沉迷 obsessed with，誘惑 tempted to，健康相關問題 health-related problems。

作文範例

①In my opinion, playing online games has its pros and cons. ②On the one hand, it ③provides people with entertainment and recreation. It is also ④a good way for teenagers and adults to relieve stress. On the other hand, playing online games can ⑤bring about harmful effects. People who ⑥are addicted to online games spend too much time on them, and this may ⑦affect their work. Many students ⑧waste precious time playing games when they should be doing something more meaningful. ⑨While most online games are free, some have purchase options, and people who are obsessed with the games may be tempted to spend ⑩more and more money. Another concern is health-related problems ⑪as staring at screens for long hours is bad for our eyesight. ⑫In conclusion, users should limit the time and money they spend on these products.

範例中譯

依我的看法，玩線上遊戲有利有弊。一方面，線上遊戲為人們提供娛樂和消遣。它也是青少年和成年人抒解壓力的好方法。另一方面，玩線上遊戲

可能帶來有害的影響。線上遊戲成癮的人花太多時間在這上面，而這可能會影響到他們的工作。許多學生在他們應該要做某些更有意義的事的時候，浪費他們寶貴的時間去玩遊戲。儘管大部分的線上遊戲是免費的，有些遊戲有加購選擇，而沉迷於遊戲的人可能會禁不起誘惑而花越來越多的錢。另一個擔憂是健康相關的問題，因為長時間盯著螢幕對視力是不好的。總而言之，使用者應該限制花在這些產品上的時間和金錢。

重點文法分析

① 說明文的結構為：開頭，正文，結論。當然，在篇幅 120 字以上的短文中，不一定要分成三個段落。開頭和結論也只需要一句話即可。由於字數和時間的限制，開頭可直接開門見山，說明這篇短文的主題，提到使用平板電腦和手機玩網路遊戲的利與弊。最簡短有力的開頭是：「依我的看法（In my opinion）」或者也可說 In my view。

② 本文的論述主要分成：使用平板電腦或手機玩網路遊戲的好處和壞處，可以用「On the one hand（一方面）、On the other hand（另一方面）」來說明，讓文章更有條理。

③ provide（提供）和介系詞 with 搭配，例如：The company provides him with a car.（公司提供他一台車子）。

④ a good way for ... to V 表示「做…的好方法」，例如：Listening to English songs is a good way for people to learn English.（聽英文歌曲是人們學英文的好方法）。

⑤ bring about（帶來），lead to（導致），cause（造成）的意思相似，可以通用。

⑥ 英文句子中經常出現 to + V 不定詞的用法，有些人會覺得 to + V-ing 動名詞怪怪的。addicted to V-ing 表示「對於『做某事』上癮」，我們可以把『做某事』想成是一個會讓你上癮的事物，所以要用 V-ing 動名詞來表示，而動名詞可理解為：把原本的動詞變成名詞的形態。其他必須加動名詞的用法有：dedicated to V-ing（盡心盡力於）、devoted to V-ing（盡心盡力於）、look forward to V-ing（期待）、when it comes to V-ing（說到）。

⑦ affect 和 effect 的中文都是「影響」，必須特別注意的是：affect 是動詞，effect 是名詞。「A 影響 B」：A affects B。「A 對 B 的影響」：The effects of A on B。如果覺得兩者容易搞混，可把 affect 的開頭 a 和 act 做聯想，act 是 action 的動詞，意思是「行動」，affect 和 act（行動）都是動詞。

⑧ 不管是 spend time（花時間）、waste time（浪費時間）或 be busy with（忙著…），後面要用動名詞 V-ing，記得「動名詞」就是把動詞變成名詞的形態來使用。

⑨ While most..., some....（儘管大部分…，但是有些還是…）記得兩個句子只能用一個連接詞，因此有 While（儘管）後面就不需要加 but（但是）。

⑩ more and more（越來越多的）同時用兩個形容詞的比較級，目的是加強語氣，例如：More and more people are keeping pets.（越來越多人飼養寵物）。The weather is getting colder and colder.（天氣變得越來越冷了）。

⑪ 若覺得用 because（因為）太簡單，可改用 as（由於）。另外一個需要注意的地方是主詞和動詞一致的原則。staring at screens for long hours（長時間盯著螢幕）是利用動名詞當主詞，一個動名詞視為單數 it，因此動詞要用 is，例如：Reading novels is interesting.（看小說是很有趣的）。雖然小說是複數，不過主詞是「看小說」這件事，只有一件事所以視為單數。

⑫ 最後一句的「總結」除了用 In conclusion，也可以用 To sum up 或 To conclude。

複試 口說測驗 解析

▶▶▶ 第一部分 朗讀短文

請先利用 1 分鐘的時間閱讀下面的短文，然後在 2 分鐘內以正常的速度，清楚正確的讀出下面的短文。

短文

A majority of Hollywood blockbuster movies have certain elements in common: romance, fantasy, thrills and comedy. Themes that bring tears to our eyes seem to be the minority. Nowadays, the audience prefers laughter to sadness. Another interesting trend is the rise of horror movies. The more frightened viewers are, the more they love it.

          *   *   *

Despite the fact that music is not one of my strengths, I still enjoy listening to songs. I can't play any musical instrument, yet I can indulge myself in graceful melodies. I know nothing about classical music, but I have a special liking for pop music. Except heavy rock, I love all kinds of music. As a writer, music is my main source of inspiration.

中譯

大部分的好萊塢賣座電影都有某些共通元素：愛情、奇幻、驚悚和喜劇。讓我們眼淚直流的主題似乎是少數。如今，觀眾比較偏好歡笑多過於哀傷。另一個有趣的趨勢是恐怖片的崛起。觀眾越是害怕，他們就越喜歡這部電影。

          *   *   *

儘管事實上音樂不是我的強項之一，我還是喜歡聽音樂。我不會彈奏任何樂器，但我卻可以讓自己沉醉在優美的旋律中。我對古典音樂一竅不通，但是我對流行音樂有特別的喜愛。除了硬式搖滾樂之外，我喜歡各式各樣的音樂。身為作家，音樂是我主要的靈感來源。

第 1 回
第 2 回
第 3 回
第 4 回
第 5 回
第 6 回

高分解析

1 重點單字：majority [məˋdʒɔrətɪ] 大部分，多數；blockbuster [ˋblɑk͵bʌstɚ] 暢銷巨作；fantasy [ˋfæntəsɪ] 幻想；thrill [θrɪl] 驚悚；comedy [ˋkɑmədɪ] 喜劇；theme [θim] 主題；minority [maɪˋnɔrətɪ] 小部分，少數；audience [ˋɔdɪəns] 觀眾；trend [trɛnd] 趨勢；horror [ˋhɔrɚ] 恐怖；frightened [ˋfraɪtn̩d] 害怕的；despite [dɪˋspaɪt] 儘管；strength [strɛŋθ] 強項，力量；instrument [ˋɪnstrəmənt] 樂器；indulge [ɪnˋdʌldʒ] 沉迷；melody [ˋmɛlədɪ] 旋律；classical [ˋklæsɪk!] 古典的；except [ɪkˋsɛpt] 除了…以外；source [sors] 來源；inspiration [͵ɪnspəˋreʃən] 靈感，啟發

2 請注意 ill 的發音，ill 的正確發音帶有短音 [ɪl] 的聲音，例如 ill，will，kill，still，以及 thrill。still 和 steal 的母音有差異，不能唸成長音 [il] 的音。

3 朗讀高分技巧

以下朗讀文章中有顏色的單字需要唸稍微大聲一點，讓語調有起伏。文章中有 | 的地方表示可以稍做停頓，讓語氣更加從容，更有自信。

A majority of Hollywood blockbuster movies | have certain elements in common: | romance, | fantasy, | thrills | and comedy. | Themes that bring tears to our eyes | seem to be the minority. | Nowadays, | the audience | prefers laughter to sadness. | Another interesting trend | is the rise of horror movies. | The more frightened viewers are, | the more they love it.

*　　　　　　*　　　　　　*

Despite the fact | that music is not one of my strengths, | I still enjoy listening to songs. | I can't play any musical instrument, | yet I can indulge myself in graceful melodies. | I know nothing about classical music, | but I have a special liking | for pop music. | Except heavy rock, | I love all kinds of music. | As a writer, | music is my main source of inspiration.

這個部分共有 10 題。題目已事先錄音，每題經由耳機播出二次，不印在試卷上。第 1 至 5 題，每題回答時間 15 秒；第 6 至 10 題，每題回答時間 30 秒。每題播出後，請立即回答。回答時，不一定要用完整的句子，但請在作答時間內儘量的表達。

1 **Do you have enough money to spend? What takes up most of your monthly budget?**

你有足夠的錢可以花嗎？每個月大部分的預算都花在什麼地方呢？

答題策略

如果你是學生，可直接說明零用錢夠不夠，零用錢有沒有包括食物和交通費，剩餘的錢會買些什麼。如果你是上班族，扣除固定開支如：房租、伙食費、通勤費、治裝費、帳單等，每個月可存多少錢，還剩下多少錢當娛樂的費用。

回答範例 1

I don't have enough pocket money. My parents give me enough allowance only for food and transport. I hardly have anything left to buy the things I like. I enjoy reading novels and comics so I rent them instead of buying them. I also borrow books from the library so I won't have to spend any money.

我沒有足夠的零用錢。我的父母只給我足夠支付食物和交通的費用。我幾乎沒剩多少錢來買我喜歡的東西。我喜歡看小說和漫畫，所以我會用租的而不是用買的。我也會從圖書館借書，這樣我就不用花任何錢。

回答範例 2

Rent alone takes up a quarter of my monthly budget. Food accounts for another 30%. After spending what I need on transport and daily necessities, I have very little left for entertainment. I try to save at least 10% of my monthly salary.

單單是房租就占用了我每個月預算的四分之一。食物用掉另外的百分之三十。扣除需要花在交通和日常必需品之後，我剩下很少的錢可以當娛樂。我努力把至少月薪的百分之十存起來。

重點補充

像口說這樣的臨場考試就像面試一樣，除非做好完全的準備，否則很難回答得既有內容又有深度。遇到這種問題不需要緊張，可以用避重就輕的方式來回答。重點是你用英文說很多內容，而且也沒有偏離主題。

Talking about money, what should I say? I would like to have more if possible, it is never enough. There is always something I want to buy, but I can't afford it. I spend a lot on food and clothes.

說到錢，我該說什麼呢？如果可能的話我當然想要更多，錢是不會有足夠的一天。總是有我想要買但是卻負擔不起的東西。我花很多錢在食物和服裝上。

2 Whom do you share your troubles with? Is it always the same person?

你會跟誰分享你的煩惱？每次都是同一個人嗎？

答題策略

為了應付這類「你會跟誰分享…」，建議先想好一個人，就算實際上沒有這個人，也可以立刻假設一個人物。例如「對你影響最大的人」、「跟你感情最好的人」、「一個你不能沒有的人」，都可以用同一個人來回答。

第 1 回
第 2 回
第 3 回
第 4 回
第 5 回
第 6 回

I have an older sister, and we are very close. I usually share my troubles with her because she listens to me patiently. Sometimes she doesn't have an answer to my problems, but I appreciate her listening to me. She is someone I can trust.

我有一個姐姐，我們感情很要好。我通常會跟她分享我的煩惱，因為她會很有耐心地聽我說。有時候我的問題她也沒有答案，但是我感謝她聽我傾訴。她是我可以信任的人。

I always complain to my friends if I have problems. It depends on who happens to be available to listen to me. We always crack some jokes, and that helps me feel better. I try not to discuss my troubles with my family because I don't want them to worry about me.

如果我有困擾，我總是跟朋友抱怨。這要看誰剛好有空聽我訴說。我們總是會開開玩笑，這樣會讓我覺得比較舒服。我儘量不跟家人討論我的煩惱，因為我不想讓他們擔心我。

重點補充

如果你真的沒有可以分憂解勞的人該怎麼辦呢？如果你是那種內向又不愛說話的人，那就照實說吧。

I always keep things to myself. There is no one I can discuss my problems with. When I am sad, I don't feel like talking. If my friends ask me what is wrong with me, I will say everything is fine. What is the use of complaining about your problems?

我總是把事情藏在心裡。沒有人可以跟我討論我的問題。當我難過時，我不想講話。如果朋友問我，我怎麼了，我會說一切都很好。跟別人抱怨你的問題有什麼用？

3 Tell me one bad habit that you have. Will you do anything about it?

告訴我一個你有的壞習慣。你將會如何處理這個壞習慣？

答題策略

雖然壞習慣跟缺點不太一樣，不過缺點有時候就是一種壞習慣造成的。一般人的壞習慣可能有咬手指甲或忘東忘西等等。咬手指甲是壞習慣，忘東忘西是壞習慣也是缺點。

回答範例 1

Well, let me think about it. I have the bad habit of biting my fingernails when I am nervous. Once, I had to go on stage to speak in front of more than a hundred people. I kept biting my fingernails as I spoke. My teacher told me I have to kick this bad habit.

嗯，讓我想一想。當我緊張的時候，我有咬手指甲的壞習慣。有一次，我必須上台在一百多人的面前講話。在我說話的時候一直咬手指甲。我的老師跟我說，我必須戒掉這個壞習慣。

回答範例 2

One of my bad habits is that I keep forgetting people's names. Sometimes I call people the wrong names, and they get angry. I think this is a bad habit I need to get rid of. Remembering people's names is a sign of respect. I have to put in more effort.

我的其中一個壞習慣是我一直忘記別人的名字。有時候我會叫錯別人的名字，他們就會生氣。我認為這是一個我必須改掉的壞習慣。記住別人的名字是一種尊重的表現。我必須更加努力才行。

重點補充

如果說自己一個壞習慣也沒有，似乎有點太完美。不過有時候就是「忽然」想不出來，這時候也可以來一招「嫁禍他人」，犧牲家裡的某個成員或任何一個朋友，並談論他們的壞習慣。

Bad habits? I'm not sure. I am not perfect, but I don't think I have any bad habits. My father likes to smoke and I hate it. It is bad for health and a waste of money. One of my friends is always late. I think that is a bad habit. She always makes excuses, and that is another bad habit.

壞習慣？我不確定（我有沒有）。我並不完美，但是我不認為我有任何壞習慣。我的爸爸喜歡抽菸，我很討厭他抽菸。抽菸不健康又浪費錢。我有一個朋友每次都遲到。 我認為這是一個壞習慣。她總是找藉口，那又是另一個壞習慣。

4 Do you enjoy vegetarian food? What makes up a healthy diet?

你喜歡吃素嗎？什麼才是健康的飲食？

答題策略

多吃蔬菜對身體有益，但喜不喜歡吃素又是另一個問題。想得到高分的話，必須運用飲食、營養方面的關鍵詞，例如 vitamins（維他命），protein（蛋白質），balanced（均衡的）。

回答範例1

Yes, my grandmother is a vegetarian so she always prepares vegetables, fruit and beans for every meal. I think vegetarian food can also be delicious. She says we can get enough vitamins and protein without having to eat meat. Personally, I think a healthy diet should be balanced.

是的，我的奶奶是吃素的人，所以她總是每一餐都準備蔬菜、水果和豆類。我認為素食也可以很美味。她說我們不用吃肉也可以得到足夠的維他命和蛋白質。就個人而言，我認為健康的飲食應該是要均衡的。

回答範例2

I don't mind eating fruit and vegetables but I don't think I can live without eating meat for a week. Meat is important as it provides the protein we need. We need to eat a variety of foods to stay healthy.

我不介意吃水果和蔬菜，但我不認為我可以一個星期不吃肉。肉類之所以重要，是因為它提供我們所需要的蛋白質。我們需要吃各式各樣的食物來保持健康。

重點補充

即便是母語人士，除非對吃的方面很講究，否則也説不出所有蔬菜的名稱。假設你很喜歡吃某種青菜，但不知道英文名稱是什麼，建議不要講。英文口試中突然冒出一句：My favorite vegetable is 大陸妹，就會對你的成績非常不利。儘量避開不會講的單字，用自己會說的方式多講幾句。

Yes, I like to eat vegetables. I like all kinds of vegetables. I usually have a salad in the morning. I also eat an apple after lunch. An apple a day keeps the doctor away. I think a healthy diet is less meat and more fruits and vegetables. French fries and fast food is not good for health.

是的，我喜歡吃蔬菜。我喜歡各種蔬菜。我早上通常吃沙拉。午餐後我會也吃一顆蘋果。一天一蘋果，醫生遠離我。我認為健康的飲食是少一點肉類，多一點水果和青菜。薯條和速食對健康是不好的。

5 Are you happy with your look? If possible, is there anything you would like to change?

你對於你的長相滿意嗎？如果有可能的話，有什麼是你想要改變的嗎？

答題策略

可能是因為不想重複往年出過的題目，口說的問題變得越來越多樣化。說自己對自己的長相很滿意的話，好像有點自戀。說自己不滿意自己的長相，又好像在說自己長得很抱歉。建議說一些很正面的話，例如外觀並不是最重要的，要接受自己，對自己有信心之類的話。

回答範例 1

I guess I am. I am not the best-looking person in the world, but I am happy with my look. I think it is important to accept our own looks and feel confident about ourselves.

我想我還算滿意。我不是世界上最好看的人，但是我對於自己的長相還算滿意。我認為接受自己的樣貌，並對自己有信心是很重要的。

I wish I were taller and thinner. I think I am a little plump so I would like to lose some weight. I would also like to make my eyes bigger and my nose smaller. However, plastic surgery is not an option for me.

我希望我可以再高一點,瘦一點。我認為我有點發福,所以我想要減肥。我也想要把我的眼睛變大一點,鼻子變小一點。然而,整形手術對我來說不是一個選擇。

重點補充

遇到這種比較特別的問題,有時候只能來個「大智若愚」,用最笨的方式來回答,別忘了只要你敢講,你有講,講得多,就能順利通過。

Let me see. I am 170 cm. I want to grow taller, but I don't think it is possible. I am 56 kg. I am too skinny. I want to have more muscles. As for my face, sometimes people say my ears are too big, but I am used to it. I am not sure what I want to change.

我看看。 我身高 170 公分。我想要再長高一點,但我認為那是不可能的。我體重 56 公斤。我太瘦了。我想要有更多肌肉。至於我的臉,有時候人們說我的耳朵太大,但是我習慣了。我不確定我想要改變什麼。

6 Do you think it is better to work overseas or get employed in Taiwan? If you have the chance to work abroad, would you take it?

你認為到國外工作比較好,或是在台灣工作比較好?如果你有機會到國外工作,你會把握機會嗎?

答題策略

如果你有考慮到國外工作,可以說一說到國外工作的好處,如果想留在台灣的話,也應該說明原因,這樣就能有足夠的表達內容。

回答範例 1

Yes, I will definitely take the chance to work overseas. It will be a great experience to work in a different country. I have never been abroad so it will be an eye-opener for me. Perhaps I can make use of my holidays to travel in that country. I love to interact with people from different cultures. The one country I have in mind is Australia because I heard that the people there are friendly. Australia is a large country with breathtaking scenery.

會的，我一定會把握到國外工作的機會。在不同的國家工作將會是一個很棒的經驗。我從來沒有出過國，所以這將讓我大開眼界。或許我可以利用假日在那個國家旅遊。我很喜歡跟來自不同文化的人們互動。我心裡想要去的國家是澳洲，因為我聽說那裡的人很友善。澳洲是個很大的國家，並擁有令人嘆為觀止的風景。

回答範例 2

I'm not sure if I want to. It will be lonely to work in a foreign country. I wonder if I will get used to the food and the climate. I went to Europe for two weeks last year, and I missed Taiwan. I missed my family, my friends and all the things that I am familiar with back home. It's all right to go on a tour but I don't think I want to work abroad. I am not an independent person.

我不確定我是否想去。在異國工作將會很寂寞。我不知道我是否能習慣那裡的食物和氣候。我去年到歐洲兩個星期，結果我很想念台灣。我想念我的家人、朋友和所有我在家鄉熟悉的所有事物。去旅行是沒什麼問題，但是我不想要到國外工作。我不是一個獨立的人。

重點補充

假設你是那種凡事都拿不定主意，總是猶豫不決的人，也可以直接說因為考量出國工作的 pros and cons（有利有弊）所以還沒下定決心。

I had thought about it, but I have not made up my mind. There are pros and cons. I can make more money and gain working experience, but I will miss my family and friends. It's hard to get a good job in Taiwan because the pay is low. How can I live with a monthly salary of 22K? I hope my English will get better so I can work in Singapore, Australia or some other countries in the future.

我曾經想過，但是我一直還沒拿定主意。這有利有弊。我可以賺更多錢，同時得到工作經驗，但是我會想念我的家人和朋友。在台灣很難找到好的工作，因為薪水很低。我要怎麼用 2 萬 2 千元的月薪生活？我希望我的英文會變得更好，這樣我在未來就可以到新加坡、澳洲或其他國家工作。

7 Should students wear school uniforms or should they be allowed to wear anything they like? What are your views on this topic?

學生應該穿制服，或是應該允許他們穿喜歡的衣服上學？你對這個話題的看法是什麼？

答題策略

遇到一些有爭議性的議題，可以依照自己的看法選邊站，不管支持或反對都可以盡情發揮。必須注意的是，你所提出的論點必須有說服力。

回答範例 1

I have nothing against students wearing school uniforms. I think it saves everyone a lot of trouble. Students don't have to worry about what to wear. By wearing the same uniform, students can develop a sense of belonging. Another issue is about school safety. School can identify strangers immediately, and this helps to make schools safer. The only concern I have is that uniforms are sold at a high price.

我不反對學生穿學校制服。我認為這省去大家很多麻煩。學生不必煩惱要穿什麼。藉由穿同樣的制服，學生可以養成一種歸屬感。另外一個議題是關於學校的安全，學校可以立刻辨識出陌生人，這有助於讓學校更安全。我唯一擔心的是制服賣得太貴。

回答範例 2

Many countries in the west do not require students to wear school uniforms. I don't see why students should be forced to buy expensive uniforms. It is an unnecessary burden. Wearing a uniform has nothing to do with studying or becoming a good student. I think a student ID card should be good enough. University students do not have to wear uniforms. I think the same rule should apply to senior and junior high schools, with the exception of elementary schools.

許多西方國家不要求學生穿制服。我不明白為什麼學生要被迫購買昂貴的制服。這是一種不必要的負擔。穿制服跟學習或成為好學生一點關係也沒有。我認為有學生證應該就夠了。大學生不需要穿制服。我認為同樣的規則應該適用於高中和國中，國小除外。

重點補充

假設你是社會人士，穿制服的年代已經離你好遠好遠，一時之間不知道要說什麼時該怎麼辦呢？其實就只要針對 uniform（制服），稍微回答同意或不同意，然後再轉移話題，只要是跟制服有關，內容就不算離題。

There is nothing wrong with wearing uniforms to school. Policemen and mailmen have to wear uniforms, too. Thinking about what to wear every day is too much trouble. Students should not worry about fashion and clothes when they go to school. They go to school to learn, not to join a fashion show.

穿制服去學校沒有什麼不對。警察和郵差也要穿制服。每天思考應該穿什麼實在太麻煩了。學生去上學時，不應該煩惱流行和衣服的事。他們是去上學是要學習，而不是去參加服裝秀。

8 Do you get along well with the people around you? Are you popular with your friends?

你和你周遭的人相處得好嗎？你受朋友歡迎嗎？

答題策略

如果只回答：「不錯，還可以。」這樣應該很難通過考試。要做到對答如流，最好的方法是舉例說明，例如提到你很好相處，可以接著說周遭的人為什麼喜歡你。如果你認為有些同學或同事不好相處，也可以加以說明。

Yes, I get along with most of the people around me. I seldom get angry with people, and I always smile. I guess that's why my friends like me. I always greet my neighbors when I see them. We have a good relationship. I won't say I am popular since I am not talented, but I think I am a likable person. It's important to understand that nobody is perfect and to learn to accept people the way they are.

是的，我跟身邊大部分的人都相處得很好。我很少生別人的氣，而且我總是微笑。我猜這是朋友之所以喜歡我的原因。當我看到鄰居時，我總是跟他們打招呼。我們的關係很要好。我不會說我很受歡迎，因為我不是很有才華的人，但我認為我是個討人喜歡的人。重要的是，明白沒有人是完美的，並學習去接受他們原來的樣子。

It depends. I have no problems with my friends, but some of my colleagues are really hard to get along with. They always complain and blame others when something goes wrong. Once, I had a big argument with them because they tried to put the blame on me when it wasn't my fault at all. I guess some people are just terrible. I try to ignore such people as much as I can.

這要看情況。我在朋友方面是沒有問題，但是有些同事真的很難相處。每當事情出差錯，他們總是在抱怨，並且把錯怪在別人頭上。有一次，我和他們大吵一架，因為他們想把完全不是我的錯來責怪我。我想有些人就是很糟糕。我試著盡量不理會這樣的人。

重點補充

假設你是那種「人人好」的大好人，回答時大可盡量誇讚自己，不用客氣。

I am an easygoing person. I get along well with almost everybody. I don't talk much, but I am a good listener. My friends always share their problems with me. I do my best to help them. As the saying goes, friends in need are friends indeed. When you help your friends who are in trouble, they will help you when you are in trouble.

我是個很隨和的人。我跟大家幾乎都相處得很好。我的話不多，但我是個很好的聆聽者。我的

朋友們總是跟我分享他們的煩惱。我盡最大的努力去幫助他們。常言道：患難見真情。當你幫助遇到困難的朋友，當你有麻煩時他們也會幫助你。

9. When was the last time you spoke to a foreigner in English? What did you talk about?

你上次跟外國人用英語交談是什麼時候？你們說了什麼？

答題策略

類似這種「上一次…是什麼時候」的問題，時間點其實並不重要。不要因為去想到底是幾月幾日而浪費時間。遇到這類問題，就先想好用 last year（去年），last month（上個月），last week（上個星期）或 a few days ago（幾天前）等特定的時間點來回答。如果真的有跟外國人用英語交談，可以大概說明談話的內容。不需要一五一十地陳述，只要大概描述一下即可，甚至可以自己編造劇情。如果從來沒跟外國人用英語交談，也不能只說沒有就結束了，必須接著說為什麼沒有此經驗，並假設有一天遇到外國人你會怎麼做。

回答範例 1

I was waiting for the bus last week when a foreigner approached me. He wanted to get to the library, but he couldn't speak or read Chinese. I told him that I was also going to the library so he could just follow me. We chatted about the funny things he encountered in Taiwan. He is from Canada, and he is here on a student exchange program. He gave me his facebook address, and I guess we will keep in touch.

上個星期我在等公車的時候，一個外國人朝我走過來。他想要到圖書館，但是他不會說、也看不懂中文。我告訴他我也要去圖書館，所以他可以跟著我一起去。我們聊到他在台灣遇到的趣事。他來自加拿大，而且他是交換學生。他給我他的臉書帳號，我想我們會繼續保持聯絡。

I have never spoken to a foreigner in English before. First of all, I hardly meet foreigners, and when I do, I am usually too shy to talk to them. They speak really fast, and that makes me nervous. What if I misunderstand what they are saying and make a fool out of myself? After taking this test, I hope to feel more confident. The next time when I meet a foreigner, I might finally have the courage to say something.

我從來沒有跟外國人用英文交談過。首先，我很少遇到外國人，而且當我遇到他們的時候，我通常會害羞到說不出話來。他們說話說得很快，這會讓我緊張。要是我會錯意讓自己出糗了該怎麼辦？經過現在這場考試之後，我希望自己更有自信。下次當我遇到外國人的時候，或許我終於有勇氣跟他們說話了。

重點補充

在很多情況下，可能是因為口音或特殊用語的關係，讓很多人聽不懂外國人在說什麼，以下是不少人的親身經歷。

Last month when I was at the night market, a foreigner asked me something but I couldn't understand. He kept saying 'restaurant' so I told him the night market is a big restaurant. He can eat whatever he likes. In the end, someone finally understood. He wanted to go to the restroom. It's hard to understand foreigners when they speak English.

上個月我在夜市的時候，一個外國人問我某件事，但是我聽不懂。他一直說「restaurant（餐廳）」，所以我就說夜市就是一個大餐廳。他可以吃任何他想吃的東西。到最後，終於有人聽懂了。他想要上洗手間。外國人說英文的時候，要聽懂還真難。

10 What would you like to receive on your birthday? Why?

生日當天你想要得到什麼？為什麼？

答題策略

這算是送分題，不過要聽清楚 receive（收到），也要注意不能離題。例如

說，一直談到生日要怎麼過，卻沒有說明自己到底想得到什麼。如果沒有想要的禮物，可以說朋友送什麼都喜歡。

回答範例 1

What else but PS5? I have been dying to get one since the first day it was launched, but the price is way beyond my budget. I can get it much easier if I pay for it in installments, but I can't afford the monthly payments. I hope my parents will buy it for me on my birthday. I kind of hinted that my PS4 is too slow, and I showed them pictures of PS5. Well, I am keeping my fingers crossed.

除了 PS5 還有什麼？自從上市的第一天，我就超想得到一台，但是價格遠遠超出了我的預算。如果用分期付款的話會更容易得到，但是我負擔不起每個月的付款。我希望我的父母會在生日那天買給我。我有點在暗示我的 PS4 太慢了，而且還給他們看了 PS5 的照片。嗯，我一直祈禱著好運降臨。

回答範例 2

I am not really sure what I want or need. I already have a computer, a tablet, a smartphone and pretty much everything I need. Nobody is going to give me a car so I won't even dare to dream about it. I never ask for a present directly because I think it is impolite. I will be happy with whatever my friends give me, even if it is just a card. Last year, a friend of mine gave me a handmade necklace, and I love it. It's the thought that counts.

我不確定我想要什麼或需要什麼。我已經有電腦、平板、智慧型手機，還有我所需要的一切。沒有人會給我車子，所以我想也不敢想。我從來不直接向別人要禮物，因為我覺得這樣是不禮貌的。朋友給我任何東西我都會很開心，就算只是一張卡片。去年，一個朋友送我一條手作項鍊，我好喜歡。禮輕情意重。

重點補充

假設家人和朋友很少為你慶生，你也從來沒收過生日禮物，可以打「悲情牌」實話實說。

Frankly speaking, I never get any birthday present from anyone. People seem to forget my birthday. The funny thing is, sometimes I forget my own birthday, too. I think my birthday is just like any other day. I am no longer a teenager. I don't want people to remind me that I am a year older on my birthday.

坦白說，我從來沒有從任何人那裡得到過生日禮物。人們似乎都會忘記我的生日。有趣的是，我自己有時候也會忘記自己的生日。我認為我的生日跟其他天沒什麼兩樣。我不再是青少年了。我不想要別人在我生日那天提醒我說我又老了一歲。

 第三部分 **看圖敘述**

> 下面有一張圖片及四個相關的問題，請在 1 分半鐘內完成作答。作答時，請直接回答，不需將題號及題目唸出。
>
> 首先請利用 30 秒的時間看圖及問題。

 1. 照片裡的人在什麼地方？
2. 照片裡的人在做什麼？
3. 照片裡的人為什麼會在那裡？
4. 如果尚有時間，請詳細描述圖片中的景物。

第 1 回
第 2 回
第 3 回
第 4 回
第 5 回
第 6 回

草稿擬定

1. 照片裡的人在什麼地方？室外 outdoor、樹林 woods、白天 daytime
2. 照片裡的人在做什麼？ 做戶外活動 do outdoor activities、健行 hiking、遛狗 walk a dog
3. 照片裡的人為什麼在這裡？享受陽光和新鮮空氣 enjoy sunshine and fresh air、放鬆 relax
4. 如果尚有時間，請詳細描述圖中的景物。人們揹後背包 people with backpack、沒有表現出疲憊 show no tiredness

高分 SOP

若按照以上提示回答問題，可能說三、四句就接不下去，請利用 Who，What，When，Where，Why 等問句來組織表達的內容。圖中的人物只有兩三個人的話，可以先從人物特寫開始描述。以此圖為例，可猜測人物大約的年齡和關係。此外，進一步說明焦點人物的穿著和隨身攜帶的物品，若人物的表情看得清楚的話，也可以加以敘述。再根據以上觀察說明他們正在做什麼，接下來會做什麼。之後針對 Why，解釋為什麼他們要這麼做。至於When，可以說一說照片拍攝的時間點可能是什麼時候。還有時間的話，可以針對 How 提出個人的看法和觀察。

必殺萬用句

1. From what I can see, this picture was taken in a...（就我所看到的，這張照片是在…時候，在…地方拍攝的）
   這是可以套用在任何一張圖片題的句型，可以先說明我們對拍攝地點的判斷，讓考官對你使用有深度的表達，留下良好的印象。

2. There are ... people in the picture. 表達「圖中有…個人」的「有」要用 There，後面要加 be 動詞，而不能說 There have＋N。

3. With + N, it is likely that... 的句型表示「有…，很有可能…」，逗號後面加上圖中的人物有了這些東西，他們會處在什麼樣的狀態。例如範文中提到 With the backpacks and their dog hiking together, it is likely that these people put high priority on recreation.（揹著背包並帶著狗一起健行，這些人可能很重視休閒）

4. I can feel that... 表示「我感覺到⋯」，這個句型可以用來表達你從圖片中所推測的事物。例如：I can feel that they care about how great it is to relax at the moment... （我可以感覺得出來，他們重視當下放鬆的美好）

5. 用「Remember, 強調的重點」的句型當作結語，讓整個敘述有一個令人印象深刻的結束。例如範文裡提到現代人需要適度休息，因此結尾可以加上 Remember, taking a break is for accomplishing a longer journey.（要記得，休息是為了走更長遠的路）

回答範例

From what I can see, this picture was taken outdoors in the daytime. There are three people in the picture, including two women and a girl. I can tell from the picture that the family is going on a trek in the woods on a sunny day. The two women might be sisters or friends who like outdoor activities. With the backpacks and their dog hiking together, it is likely that these people put a high priority on recreation. With no stick for walking or towel around their necks, the people in the picture are enjoying the sunshine and the fresh air during their hike, showing no sign of tiredness. I can feel that they care about how great it is to relax at the moment instead of how fast or how far they should go. Nowadays, leisure activities are more and more important because people are under too much pressure from work or school, and they need to find ways to wind down. Remember, taking a break is for accomplishing a longer journey.

範例中譯

就我所看到的，這張照片是在白天的戶外所拍攝的。照片中有三個人，包括兩位女性及一位小女孩；我可以從照片中看出，這一家人正利用好天氣在樹林裡健行。這兩位女性可能是喜歡戶外活動的姊妹或朋友。背著背包並帶著狗一起健行，這群人很有可能十分重視休閒；他們沒有拿登山杖，脖子也沒掛毛巾，照片裡的這些人在健行途中享受著陽光及新鮮空氣，絲

毫沒有表現出疲態。我可以感覺得出來，他們重視當下放鬆的美好，而不在乎走得多快或多遠。今日，由於人們在工作或課業上的壓力太大，他們需要找到方法紓壓，因此休閒活動越來越重要。要記得，休息是為了走更長遠的路。

第 1 回
第 2 回
第 3 回
第 4 回
第 5 回
第 6 回

第三回　寫作能力測驗答題注意事項

1. 本測驗共有兩部分。第一部分為中譯英，第二部分為英文作文。測驗時間為 40 分鐘。

2. 請利用試題紙空白處背面擬稿，但正答務必書寫在「寫作能力測驗答案紙」上。在答案紙以外的地方作答，不予計分。

3. 第一部分中譯英請在答案紙第一頁作答，第二部分英文作文請在答案紙第二頁作答。

4. 作答時請勿隔行書寫，請注意字跡清晰可讀，並保持答案紙之清潔，以免影響評分。

5. 測驗時，不得在准考證或其他物品上抄題，亦不得有傳遞、夾帶小抄、左顧右盼或交談等違規行為。

6. 意圖或已經將試題紙攜出試場者，五年內不得報名參加本測驗。請人代考者，連同代考者，三年內不得報名參加本測驗。

7. 測驗結束時，須立即停止作答，在原位靜候監試人員收回全部試題紙及答案紙，清點無誤後，宣佈結束始可離場。

8. 應試者入場、出場及測驗中如有違反上列規則或不服監試人員之指示者，監試人員得取消應試資格並請其離場，且作答不予計分。

全民英語能力分級檢定測驗

中級寫作能力測驗

本測驗共有兩部份。第一部份為中譯英，第二部份為英文寫作。測驗時間為 40 分鐘。

一、中譯英 (40%)

說明：請將下列的一段中文翻譯成通順、達意且前後連貫的英文。

　　　　繪畫是一種不需要特別天分的娛樂和消遣。它所需要的只是一些簡單的工具和材料。因此，大部分的人都能享受繪畫的樂趣。無論你是初學者或職業畫家，都沒有關係。技術是隨著不斷的練習而來的。常言道：「熟能生巧」。

二、英文作文 (60%)

請依下面所提供的文字提示寫一篇英文作文，長度約 120 字（8 至 12 個句子）。作文可以是一個完整的段落，也可以分段。（評分重點包括內容、組織、文法、用字遣詞、標點符號、大小寫。）

提示：假設你有一位表妹因為和學校的同學相處得不好而苦惱，甚至因為自己沒有合得來的好友而十分憂鬱。請試著寫信去開導她。在信中你可以先安慰她，並告訴她和同學相處的一些技巧。

5

10

15

20

25

30

35

40

第三回　口說能力測驗答題注意事項

1. 本測驗問題由耳機播放，回答則經麥克風錄下。分朗讀短文、回答問題與看圖敘述三部分，時間共約 15 分鐘，連同口試說明時間共需約五十分鐘。

2. 第一部份朗讀短文有 1 分鐘準備時間，此時請勿唸出聲音，待聽到「請開始朗讀」2 分鐘的朗讀時間開始時，再將短文唸出來。第二部分回答問題的題目將播出 2 遍，聽完第二次題目後要立即回答。第三部份看圖敘述有 30 秒的思考時間及 1 分 30 秒的答題時間，思考時不可在試題紙上作記號，亦不可出聲。等聽到指示開始回答時，請您針對圖片盡量的回答。

3. 錄音設備皆已事先完成設定，請勿觸動任何機件，以免影響錄音。測驗時請戴妥耳機，將麥克風調到嘴邊約三公分處，聽清楚說明，依指示以適中音量回答。

4. 評分人員將根據您錄下的回答（發音與語調、語法與字彙、可解度及切題度等）作整體的評分。您可利用所附光碟自行測試，一一錄下回答後，再播出來聽聽，並斟酌調整。練習時請盡量以英語思考、應對，考試時較易有自然的表現。

5. 請注意測試時不可在試題紙上劃線、打「√」或作任何記號；不可在准考證或其他物品上抄題；亦不可有傳遞、夾帶小抄、左顧右盼或交談等違規行為。

6. 意圖或已將試題紙或試題影音資料攜出或傳送出試場者，視同侵犯本中心著作財產權，限五年內不得報名參加「全民英檢」測驗。請人代考，連同代考者，三年內不得報名參加本測驗。

7. 測驗結束時，須立即停止作答，在原位靜候監試人員收回全部試題紙且清點無誤後，等候監試人員宣布結束後始可離場。

8. 入場、出場及測驗中如有違反規則或不服監試人員指示者，監試人員將取消您的應試資格並請您離場，且作答不予計分，亦不退費。

全民英語能力分級檢定測驗

中級口說能力測驗

請在 15 秒內完成並唸出下列自我介紹的句子：

My seat number is （座位號碼後 5 碼）, and my registration number is （考試號碼後 5 碼）.

第一部分：朗讀短文

　　請先利用 1 分鐘的時間閱讀下面的短文，然後在 2 分鐘內以正常的速度，清楚正確的讀出下面的短文，閱讀時請不要發出聲音。

　　It is unbelievable that there are more than a hundred channels to choose from on the cable TV. We are simply spoiled for choice. The old saying goes, "What you see is what you get." Parents should keep this saying in mind. If we allow our kids to watch any channel they prefer, chances are that they will select certain programs that are unhealthy and undesirable.

＊　　　　　　　　＊　　　　　　　　＊

　　It takes a lot of sacrifice to be a top athlete. Apart from countless hours of practice and hard work, sports players are also required to keep their diet under control. This takes a great deal of willpower and discipline. Famous athletes are expected to maintain a positive image and set a good example. Quite a few celebrities ruined their reputation as a result of drug addiction.

第二部分：回答問題

　　這個部分共有 10 題。題目已事先錄音，每題經由耳機播出二次，不印在試卷上。第一至五題，每題回答時間 15 秒；第六至十題，每題回答時間 30 秒。每題播出後，請立即回答。回答時，不一定要用完整的句子，但請在作答時間內盡量的表達。

第三部分：看圖敘述

　　下面有一張圖片及四個相關的問題，請在 1 分半鐘內完成作答。作答時，請直接回答，不需將題號及題目唸出。

　　首先請利用 30 秒的時間看圖及問題。

提示：
1. 照片裡的人在什麼地方？
2. 照片裡的人在做什麼？
3. 照片裡的人為什麼會在那裡？
4. 如果尚有時間，請詳細描述圖片中的景物。

請將下列自我介紹的句子再唸一遍：

My seat number is（座位號碼後 5 碼）, and my registration number is（考試號碼後 5 碼）.

複試 寫作測驗 解析

▶▶▶ 第一部分 **中譯英** (40%)

請將下列的一段中文翻譯成通順、達意且前後連貫的英文。

繪畫是一種不需要特別天分的娛樂和消遣。它所需要的只是一些簡單的工具和材料。因此，大部分的人都能享受繪畫的樂趣。無論你是初學者或職業畫家，都沒有關係。技術是隨著不斷的練習而來的。常言道：「熟能生巧」。

翻譯範例

Painting is a form of entertainment and recreation which doesn't require special talents. All it takes is just some simple tools and materials. Therefore, most people are able to enjoy the joy and fun of painting. Whether you are an amateur or a professional painter, it doesn't matter. Skill comes with constant practice. As the saying goes, "Practice makes perfect."

逐句說明

1. 繪畫是一種不需要特別天分的娛樂和消遣。

Painting is a form of entertainment and recreation which doesn't require special talents.

這句翻譯用了形容詞子句，也就是關係代名詞 which 後面所引導的子句。形容詞子句其實就是為了和主要子句合併為一句。若不用形容詞子句的話，句子會拆成兩句寫成：Painting is a form of entertainment and recreation. 和 It doesn't require special talents. ，it 是指 painting（繪畫）。當然，會運用形容詞子句就能大大提升表達能力，其實也不是很難，只要把代名詞 It 換成關係代名詞 which，然後把兩個句子合併在一起，which doesn't require special talents 就成了形容詞子句。

除了「... a form of」，也可以用 a kind of 或 a type of 來表示「一

種…」。form 是「形式」，比較適合用於表達抽象的藝術形態。例如：Rap is a form of music.（饒舌是一種音樂形態）。recreation 和 leisure 是近義字，有消遣和休閒的涵義。然而，這兩個單字在表達時還是有慣用的搭配方式。例如： What do you do for recreation?（你做什麼來當作消遣？）。「休閒中心」是 recreation center，「休閒活動」是 recreational activities。以及 What do you do in your leisure time?（你在休閒的時候會做什麼？），He walked leisurely along the river.（他悠閒地沿著河邊走。）。

可數名詞與不可數名詞應該說只是個原則，並非硬性的規則。talent（才華，天賦）同時是可數名詞和不可數名詞，例如：He has a talent for art.（他對藝術有天分。），He is a man of many talents.（他是個多才多藝的人。）也可以指人才，例如：foreign talent（外來人才）。

2. 它所需要的只是一些簡單的工具和材料。

All it takes is just some simple tools and materials.

All S V is...（所需要的只是…）是常見的句型，be 動詞後面的主詞補語可以用名詞或不定詞，不定詞的 to 通常會省略，因此也可以直接加原形動詞，變成 All S V is (to) V。例如：All it takes is a little patience.（所需要的只是一點耐心）。All I want is have a stable job.（我所要的只是有一份穩定的工作。）All S V is 的句型在功能上和 What S V is... 有異曲同工之妙，文法規則也一樣。What I need now is a little more time.（我現在所需要的是多一點時間。）。

3. 因此，大部分的人都能享受繪畫的樂趣。

Therefore, most people are able to enjoy the joy and fun of painting.

書面寫作時要用比較正式的用詞，若用「so 所以」，看起來和聽起來都不夠正式，therefore 是比較好的選擇。寫作想拿高分，在修辭方面必須下點功夫，不只是把意思翻譯出來就好了，句子也要通順。從這個角度思考，翻譯成 are able to enjoy 比 can enjoy 來得更好。

4. 無論你是初學者或職業畫家，都沒有關係。

Whether you are an amateur or a professional painter, it doesn't matter.

Whether 子句是名詞子句，通常會用在句尾，因此這句話也可以這麼

寫：It doesn't matter whether you are an amateur or a professional painter. 這樣看來，其實把名詞子句挪到句首反而會比較好翻譯，例如：Whether you are rich or poor, it doesn't matter.（無論你有錢或沒錢，都不重要）。可以和下面這句比較：It doesn't matter whether you have a house or not.（無論你有沒有房子都不重要）。

5. 技術是隨著不斷的練習而來的。

Skill comes with constant practice.

「某個東西隨著另一個東西而來」，英文會用 come(s) with 來表達，例如：Most cellphones nowadays come with cameras.（現在大部分的手機都配有相機）。

6. 常言道：「熟能生巧」。

As the saying goes, "Practice makes perfect."

要引述成語或俚語時，可以用 As the saying goes 來做開頭，像是「常言道」、「俗話說」、「正所謂」，都能這麼翻譯。Practice makes perfect.（多練習就會完美。）是英文版的「熟能生巧」。

▶▶▶ 第二部分 英文作文 (60%)

請依下面所提供的文字提示寫一篇英文作文，長度約 120 字（8 至 12 個句子）。作文可以是一個完整的段落，也可以分段。

提示 假設你有一位表妹因為和學校的同學相處得不好而苦惱，甚至因為自己沒有合得來的好友而十分憂鬱。請試著寫信去開導她。在信中你可以先安慰她，並告訴她和同學相處的一些技巧。

結構預設

書信分為正式和非正式，本題要考生寫一封書信給表妹，屬於非正式書信，在格式上不需要太過拘謹。影響考官打分主要的還是內容。書信的第一句通常是問候語，例如問對方最近好嗎？是否別來無恙？根據提示，第一段可先安慰對方，再提出和同學相處的一些技巧。

第 1 回

第 2 回

第 3 回

第 4 回

第 5 回

第 6 回

草稿擬定

1. 問候語：How have you been?（最近如何？）
2. 點出問題：lack confidence（缺乏自信），feel inferior（感到自卑）
3. 提出建議：tips（提示；建議），humble（謙卑），modest（謙虛），put yourself in another person's shoe（設身處地為別人著想）。

作文範例

①January 10

Dear Amy,

How have you been? I ②heard from your mom that things are not going well for you. I faced a similar situation a few years ago so I can understand how you feel right now.

I think you ③lack confidence, and you always believe that people don't like you. You shouldn't ④feel this way. ⑤There is nothing wrong with you. You don't have to feel inferior. ⑥Here are a few tips you can try. Smile more often. If you smile at people sincerely, most of them will ⑦return the smile. Be humble and modest. Don't say things that might make your friends angry. Always try to ⑧put yourself in another person's shoes. Do for other people what you would like them to do for you.

I hope things will get better for you. I wish you all the best!
Your cousin,
Eric

範例中譯

一月十日

親愛的 Amy：
最近如何？我聽妳媽媽說妳過得不是很順利。幾年前我遇到相似的處境，所以我可以理解妳現在的感受。

我認為妳缺乏自信，而妳總是認為別人不喜歡妳。妳不應該這樣覺得。妳

根本就沒有做錯什麼。妳不需要感到自卑。這裡有一些建議，妳可以試試看。更常微笑。如果妳對別人真誠地微笑，大部分的人也會對妳微笑。要謙卑和謙虛。不要說一些也許會讓朋友生氣的事情。要一直試著設身處地為他人著想。妳希望別人為妳做些什麼事，妳就為他們做那些事情。

我希望妳可以過得愈來愈順利，祝妳好運！
妳的表哥 Eric

重點文法分析

① 一般書信會在信紙的右上角寫上日期，如 January 10，也常簡寫成 Jan. 10，非正式的信件中，年份通常省略；正式的書信則會寫上年代，同時把發信者的機構名稱、信件的編號、機構的住址寫在日期上方。由於本題的收件對象設定為各位考生的「表妹」，無須太過正式。依照台灣人的習慣，自己和對方的地址都寫在信封上，因此信件中就無須再重複。非正式書信的稱呼語可直接用對方的名字（first name）如：Dear Amy，正式書信則要用對方的姓氏（last name, family name, surname）前面加上 Mr.（先生）、Mrs.（夫人）或 Miss（小姐）的尊稱。結尾會表明自己的身分，例如：Your friend,（你的朋友），Your student,（你的學生）。比較親密的朋友則可以用 Yours truly,（你的摯友）。一般生意往來可用 Best wishes 或 Best regards 做為結尾語。舊式的書信格式會把結尾語寫在右下方，不過有了電子郵件後，結尾語通常會寫在左下方。

② 「從某人那聽說」用 hear from someone，不過 hear from 的另外一個意思是「聽到某人的音訊」，例如：I haven't heard from her since then.（從那時候就沒有她的消息）。hear of 則是「聽過某件事」的意思，例如：Have you heard of this place?（你聽過這個地方嗎？）

③ lack（缺乏）是及物動詞，後面要加受詞。以「自信」作為受詞時，要用名詞 confidence。confident（有自信的）則是形容詞，以下是相似的形容詞、名詞形式。
形容詞：different（不同的），important（重要的），relevant（相關的）
名詞：difference（差異），importance（重要性），relevance（關聯性）

④ way 表示「方向」和「方法」，可用於：go this way（往這邊走），feel this way（這樣覺得），In this way（這樣）。

⑤ What's wrong? 是指「怎麼了？有問題嗎？」，而 something's wrong 表示

「某事出了問題」，例如：There's something wrong with the TV.（電視機出了問題）。there's nothing wrong 表示「某事沒有問題」的意思，例如：There's nothing wrong with your attitude.（你的態度沒有問題）。

⑥ 倒裝句經常用 Here 開頭，把原本的 There is a pen here 改寫為 Here is a pen，目的是省略掉沒有具體意思的 There。一個重要的原則是：主詞為「名詞」時，可用倒裝句，但主詞為「代名詞」時，則不能用倒裝句。

倒裝句用 V + S：Here are a few tips.（這裡有一些建議）、Here comes the bus.（公車來了）

不可倒裝的句子用 S + V：Here they are.（他們來了）、Here it comes.（它來了）

⑦ 用 return 表示「歸還他人某物」時，受詞除了可以是具體的物品（如錢、書本），也可以是抽象的概念，例如：I will return the favor someday.（我有一天會還這個人情）。return the smile 字面上是「還別人的微笑」，也就是指「你對別人微笑，別人也會對你微笑」的意思。

⑧ 寫作時若能套用一兩句英文慣用語或俗語，有助於讓內容更加生動，同時也能展現英文實力。像是 If I were in your shoes（如果我是你的話），以及字面上為「把自己放在別人的鞋子裡」的 put yourself in another person's shoes 表示「從別人角度去體會他們的感受和想法」。「己所不欲、勿施於人」的英文是 Do unto others as you would have them do unto yourself.，字面上是「自己想得到什麼樣的待遇，就要用這種方式對待別人」。比較白話的寫法是，Do for other people what you would like them to do for you.。

▶▶▶ 第一部分 朗讀短文

請先利用 1 分鐘的時間閱讀下面的短文，然後在 2 分鐘內以正常的速度，清楚正確的讀出下面的短文。

短文

It is unbelievable that there are more than a hundred channels to choose from on the cable TV. We are simply spoiled for choice. The old saying goes, "What you see is what you get." Parents should keep this saying in mind. If we allow our kids to watch any channel they prefer, chances are that they will select certain programs that are unhealthy and undesirable.

*   *   *

It takes a lot of sacrifice to be a top athlete. Apart from countless hours of practice and hard work, sports players are also required to keep their diet under control. This takes a great deal of willpower and discipline. Famous athletes are expected to maintain a positive image and set a good example. Quite a few celebrities ruined their reputation as a result of drug addiction.

中譯

有線電視上有超過一百台的頻道可以選擇，這是很令人難以置信的事。我們被太多的選擇寵壞了。有句俗諺說：「所見即所得。」家長們應該把這句諺語謹記在心。如果我們允許我們的孩子觀看他們喜歡的任何頻道，可能發生的情況是，他們很有可能會選擇某些不健康和不理想的節目。

　　　　*　　　　　　　*　　　　　　　*

要成為頂尖的運動員，需要做出很多犧牲。除了無數個小時的練習和努力之外，運動選手也必須控制他們的飲食。這需要很大的意志力和自律。知名運動員也被要求維持正面的形象，並樹立良好的典範。有好幾位有名的運動員因為染上毒癮，而毀掉了他們的聲譽。

高分解析

1 重要單字：unbelievable [ˌʌnbɪˈlivəbl] 難以置信的；channel [ˈtʃænl] 頻道；spoiled [spɔɪlt] 被寵壞的，壞掉的；select [səˈlɛkt] 挑選；program [ˈprogræm] 節目；unhealthy [ʌnˈhɛlθɪ] 不健康的；undesirable [ˌʌndɪˈzaɪrəbl] 不理想的；sacrifice [ˈsækrəˌfɪs] 犧牲；athlete [ˈæθlit] 運動員；countless [ˈkaʊntlɪs] 無數的；required [rɪˈkwaɪrd] 必須的；discipline [ˈdɪsəplɪn] 紀律，自律；expect [ɪkˈspɛkt] 期待，要求；maintain [menˈten] 維持；positive [ˈpɑzətɪv] 正面的；image [ˈɪmɪdʒ] 形象；example [ɪgˈzæmpl] 例子，榜樣；celebrity [sɪˈlɛbrətɪ] 藝人，公眾人物；ruined [ˈruɪnd] 毀掉的；reputation [ˌrɛpjəˈteʃən] 名譽，聲譽；drug addiction 毒癮

2 到底全民英檢的朗讀短文部分時要不要使用連音或縮寫的唸法，例如 it is 是不是要唸成 [ɪt_ɪs] 或 it's，we are 要不要唸成 we're，其實見仁見智，也不一定會被扣分，但是這樣唸卻有潛在的風險，因為我們畢竟不是母語人士，連音不見得會連得漂亮，而且朗讀短文的部分不但有足夠的時間把每個字唸清楚，短文也不會用縮寫形式呈現，為了追求穩健拿分，這方面的技巧還是不要過度使用為宜。

3 朗讀高分技巧
以下朗讀文章中有顏色的單字需要唸稍微大聲一點，讓語調有起伏。文章中有 | 的地方表示可以稍做停頓，讓語氣更加從容，更有自信。

It is unbelievable | that there are more than a hundred channels | to choose from on the cable TV. | We are simply spoiled for choice. | The old saying goes, | "What you see | is what you get." | Parents should keep this saying in mind. | If we allow our kids | to watch any channel they prefer, | chances are | that they will select certain programs | that are unhealthy | and undesirable.

*   *   *

It takes a lot of sacrifice | to be a top athlete. | Apart from countless hours of practice | and hard work, | sports players are also required | to keep their diet under control. | This takes a great deal of willpower and discipline. | Famous athletes are expected to maintain a positive image and set a good example. | Quite a few celebrities | ruined their reputation | as a result of drug addiction.

▶▶▶ 第二部分 回答問題

> 這個部分共有 10 題。題目已事先錄音,每題經由耳機播出二次,不印在試卷上。第 1 至 5 題,每題回答時間 15 秒;第 6 至 10 題,每題回答時間 30 秒。每題播出後,請立即回答。回答時,不一定要用完整的句子,但請在作答時間內儘量的表達。

1 **Do you believe that there are aliens? Why or why not?**

你相信有外星人嗎?為什麼相信?為什麼不相信?

答題策略

請注意,題目問的外星人是指真的外星物種,並且詢問相信或不相信的原因。如果你看過 ET(Extra-terrestrial 來自外太空)或其他關於外星人的電

影，應該可以回答這個問題。除了說明自己的立場，記得也要說明為什麼相信或不相信。

回答範例 1

Yes, I believe there are aliens because the universe is so vast. There is a high possibility of life on another planet. I don't think they will look like humans. I have always been fascinated by UFOs and aliens. I hope scientists can prove that aliens are real.

是的，我相信有外星人，因為宇宙如此浩瀚。在另外一個星球上有生命的存在是極有可能的。我不認為他們會長得像人類。我一直都對幽浮和外星人很感興趣。我希望科學家可以證實外星人是真實存在的。

回答範例 2

I don't think so. There is a lot of speculation going around but I don't buy the story. According to some scientists, life on earth is a pure miracle. There can't be any intelligent life-form on other planets as they are either too hot or too cold.

我不這麼認為。目前有很多的揣測，但是我不相信。根據一些科學家的說法，地球上有生命是一件奇蹟。其他星球上不太可能存在任何有智慧的生命型態，因為這些星球不是太熱，就是太冷。

重點補充

萬一錄音播太快，或者沒聽懂 aliens 這個單字該怎麼辦？在萬不得已的情況下，雖然聽不懂還是可以用「顧左右而言他」的方式，來回答類似「你相信⋯嗎？」的問題。

This is a tough question. It's really hard to say. Some people believe it while others don't. I have never seen one myself, so I don't really believe it. However, it might be true. I hope someone can prove it soon.

這是個很難的問題。這真的很難說。有些人相信，但其他人卻不信。我自己從來沒看過，所以我不相信。然而，這也有可能是真的。我希望有人可以證實這件事。

第 1 回
第 2 回
第 3 回
第 4 回
第 5 回
第 6 回

Have you ever watched the sunrise? If not, would you like to do so in the future?

你曾經欣賞過日出嗎？如果沒有的話，你未來會想去看嗎？

答題策略

就算自己沒親眼看過，總看過新聞報導「新的一年第一道曙光」之類的照片吧。如果看過的話，要補充說明是在哪裡看的，並對日出的畫面加以形容。沒看過的話也沒關係，可直接說沒看過，並說明原因，也可以把話題轉移到看過日落的經驗。

回答範例 1

Last summer I went to Alishan with my friends. We watched the sunrise early in the morning. It was beautiful beyond words. Though I had to get up early to watch it, I think it was worth the effort. I was glad I didn't miss it. We took a lot of amazing pictures.

去年夏天我跟朋友去了阿里山。我們在一大早看了日出。日出的美簡直無法用文字形容。雖然我為了看日出必須早起，但我認為這樣的努力是值得的。我很高興我沒有錯過日出。我們拍了很多很棒的照片。

回答範例 2

I have never seen the sunrise yet, but I saw the sunset a few times. I am too lazy to get up so early in the morning. I think the sunset is more beautiful. You can see the clouds change colors, and it is more romantic. Perhaps I will try to get up early some day.

我沒有看過日出，但是我倒是看過幾次日落。我太懶了，所以沒辦法這麼早起。我認為日落比較美。你可以看到雲朵的顏色變換，而且比較浪漫。或許某天我會試著早起。

重點補充

回答的情境也有可能是原本想看，結果沒看成，反正只要跟日出有關，都是可以接受的內容。

Last year, I went to Hualien with my family during the winter vacation. My mom woke me up at 4:30 a.m. It was freezing cold. We waited for more than an hour, but we didn't see the sun rise. It was too foggy.

去年，我在寒假時和家人到花蓮。我媽在凌晨四點半把我叫醒。那時冷得要命。我們等了超過一個小時，但是沒看到日出。因為霧太濃了。

3 What do you usually do when you are waiting for someone or something?

你在等待某個人或某件事的時候，通常會做什麼？

答題策略

現在的人最喜歡做什麼？當然是滑手機。在等人或等東西的時候，大部分的人都會用手機或平板來打發時間。當然，你也可以反其道而行，做個不愛滑手機的人。不滑手機能做什麼呢？看看小說或複習筆記吧。

回答範例 1

I guess I will take out my cellphone and play a game with it. Isn't that what everyone else does when they are on the bus or the train? Sometimes I listen to my favorite songs or take a look at the pictures I took with my cellphone.

我想我會拿出我的手機、玩個遊戲。大家在公車上或火車上不都會這樣做嗎？有時候我會聽我最喜歡的歌曲，或看看我用手機拍的照片。

回答範例 2

If I happen to carry a novel with myself, I will read it. Most of the time, I review my notes because I need to remember a lot of information. Time is precious to me so I try to make full use of it.

如果我剛好有帶一本小說在身上，那我會讀那本小說。大部分的時候我都會複習我的筆記，因為我需要記很多資訊。時間對我來說很珍貴，所以我都會試著善加利用。

重點補充

如果你不滑手機也不讀東西，在等待的時候就是腦袋放空、胡思亂想，不然就是觀察身邊的人在做什麼，也可以照實表達。

Well, what exactly do I do? I will just daydream about something or think about the things I have to do later. Sometimes I just observe the people around me and listen to their conversations.

嗯，我到底會做什麼呢？我只會做白日夢，或者想一想等一下要做的事情。有時候，我只是觀察身邊的人，聽一聽他們的對話。

4 What are you afraid of? Are you afraid of certain insects?

你害怕什麼？你怕某些昆蟲嗎？

答題策略

說到害怕的東西，這個範圍很廣，本題把範圍縮小，只問你怕不怕昆蟲。如果怕蟑螂或其他昆蟲，可直接說明，並解釋害怕的原因，例如提到某一次的遭遇。

回答範例 1

I am terrified of cockroaches, especially those that can fly. I think they are disgusting. Once, a cockroach got on my neck, and I screamed. Fortunately, my brother killed it for me.

我很怕蟑螂，特別是那些會飛的。我認為牠們很噁心。有一次，一隻蟑螂跑到我的脖子，害我大聲尖叫。幸好，我哥哥幫我把牠打死了。

第1回
第2回
第3回
第4回
第5回
第6回

回答範例 2

I am not afraid of insects. In fact, I find them interesting. I am afraid of the dark. I always sleep with the bathroom light on. I guess it's because of all those horror films I watched.

我不害怕昆蟲。事實上，我覺得昆蟲很有趣。我怕黑。我睡覺時，浴室的燈總是要開著。我想這是因為我看過的那些恐怖片的緣故。

重點補充

或許你是天不怕地不怕，天塌下來當被子蓋的無敵英雄，不過要這樣回答有點難度。如果想不到害怕的昆蟲，也可以轉移話題，談一談其他讓你擔心的事情。

I am not afraid of any insects or animals. However, I am worried about my future. Houses are so expensive now. I don't think I can afford to buy a house in Taipei.

我不害怕任何昆蟲或動物。然而，我很擔心我的未來。房子現在這麼貴。我不認為我在台北能夠買得起房子。

5 Are you curious about science and nature? What makes you curious?

你對科學和大自然感到好奇嗎？什麼讓你好奇？

答題策略

即使平常很少看與科學、大自然相關的影片，在談話中能夠提到一些英語的教育頻道，會有加分效果。National Geographic Channel（國家地理頻道），Animal Planet（動物星球），Discovery Channel（探索頻道）。如果對科學沒興趣，也不知道針對科學可以說什麼，那麼另外說一個自己感興趣的事物也是可行的。

回答範例 1

I have always been curious about stars and planets. I love to watch programs on Discovery Channel. I think it is incredible how scientists know so much about the universe.

我一直以來對星星和行星都很好奇。我喜歡看探索頻道的節目。我認為科學家知道這麼多關於宇宙的事情，真的是很不可思議。

回答範例2

I am curious about cooking. Cooking may not be a science, but to me it is an art. There is a lot to learn about making dishes. It is not as easy as it seems to be.

我對烹飪感到好奇。烹飪或許不算一門科學，但對我來說，烹飪是一門藝術。關於做菜有很多東西要學。它不是像看起來的那麼容易。

重點補充

萬一你對科學都沒興趣，對大自然都不好奇，就談談自己的興趣吧。

I am not curious about science. In fact, I am not curious about anything. My friends always say I am a boring person. My only interest is reading comics.

我對科學不感到好奇。事實上，我不對任何事物感到好奇。我的朋友總是說我是個無趣的人。我唯一的興趣是看漫畫。

6 Do you think it is better to drive a car or take public transport?

你認為開車或是搭乘大眾運輸比較好？

答題策略

開車或坐大眾運輸都有優缺點，可根據自己的真實情況說明你認為哪一個比較好。開車的好處是想去哪裡就去哪裡，特別是在下雨天會比較方便。捷運站和公車站不是每個地方都有，但是坐捷運或公車便宜、快速、方便又環保，也是不錯的選擇。

回答範例1

I prefer to drive a car because public transport is always crowded during rush hours. Although it costs more to drive a car, I think it is more convenient, especially on rainy days. There is no MRT station near my house, so driving a car is a better option. With a family car, we can travel to many places in Taiwan to have a vacation. The only concern I have is the high petrol price.

我比較喜歡開車，因為大眾運輸在尖峰時刻總是很擁擠。雖然開車要花比較多錢，但我認為開車比較方便，尤其是在下雨天。我的住家附近沒有捷運站，所以開車是比較好的選擇。有一部家用車，我們可以到台灣的許多地方去度假。我唯一的顧慮就是高油價。

第 1 回
第 2 回
第 3 回
第 4 回
第 5 回
第 6 回

回答範例 2

It is definitely better to take public transport. I find the MRT system in Taipei convenient and reliable. Taking the MRT is also much faster than driving a car, and you don't have to worry about parking. Taking public transport also helps to save the earth, as cars produce air pollution. I hope more and more people take public transport instead of driving cars or riding motorcycles.

搭乘大眾運輸肯定是比較好的。我覺得台北的捷運系統既方便，又很可靠。坐捷運也比開車還快，而且不需要擔心停車的問題。搭乘大眾運輸也有助於拯救地球，因為車子會造成空氣汙染。我希望越來越多人改搭大眾運輸，而不是開車或騎機車。

重點補充

假設你是學生，通常的情況是爸媽騎機車載你上下課，你也可以照實說。

My mom rides a motorcycle. She sends me to school every day. My school is not near any MRT station. I can take the bus but my mom says it is faster and more convenient to ride a motorcycle. When I am old enough, I want to drive a car. It's cool to have a car. I can go anywhere I want.

我的媽媽騎機車。她每天載我去上課。我的學校附近沒有任何捷運站。我可以搭公車，但是媽媽說騎機車比較快，也比較方便。當我年紀夠大時，我想要開車。有一台車子很酷。我想去哪裡都可以。

7

Have you ever taken part in a competition? If not, what kind of competition would you like to take part in?

你參加過任何比賽嗎？如果沒有的話，你會想參加什麼樣的比賽？

答題策略

這題有點難度，假設你參加的是大胃王比賽，一時之間很難翻譯成英文吧？建議用演講、歌唱或寫作這類比較好講的比賽來回答。可以回顧當初比賽的情境，準備的過程和得獎的心情。如果從來沒有參加過比賽，也想不出什麼比賽，就坦白地承認，並說明沒有參加的原因。

回答範例 1

Yes, I took part in a speech competition when I was in elementary school. I still remember what I talked about that day. My teacher spent a lot of time training me. I kept repeating the same speech for at least a hundred times. Though I was nervous, I managed to finish it, and I got second place. It was a memorable experience. Public speaking is an important skill.

有的，我在國小時參加過演講比賽。我還記得我那天說了什麼。我的老師花了很多時間訓練我。我一直重複一樣的演說至少一百次。雖然我很緊張，我還是完成了演講，並得到第二名。那是一個難忘的經驗。公開演講是一個很重要的技能。

回答範例 2

Not that I can remember. Perhaps I took part in games and quizzes before but I have never signed up for any formal competition. I am a shy person, so I don't think I am up to it. I always admire people who have the courage to sing in front of an audience. I wonder how they overcome their fears. I can't even speak properly if I face the camera.

我記得好像沒有。或許我之前參加過遊戲和問答比賽，但我從來沒有報名參加過任何正式的比賽。我是個害羞的人，所以我覺得我辦不到。我總是很佩服那些有勇氣在觀眾面前唱歌的人。我不曉得他們是如何克服他們的恐懼。如果我面對鏡頭，我甚至連話都說不好。

重點補充

假設你有慘痛的經驗，也可以大方說出來，畢竟不是所有比賽都能得獎。

I took part in a singing competition once. It was Mother's Day. I wanted to sing a song to thank my mom. I practiced many times but when I got on the stage, I forgot some of the words (lyrics). It was embarrassing. I didn't win any prize, but my mom said she was touched.

有一次我參加歌唱比賽。那天是母親節。我想要唱一首歌來感謝媽媽。我練習了很多次，但是當我一上台，我就忘了一些字（歌詞），這真丟臉。我沒有贏得任何獎品，但是媽媽說她很感動。

8 What's your mother like? How will you describe her?

你母親是個怎樣的人？你會如何形容她？

答題策略

請特別注意，這題問的是 What's... like，你母親是個怎樣的人，而不是 What does... like，你母親喜歡什麼。雖然形容媽媽的外貌和長相也不能算錯，不過依照題目的要求，主要是問媽媽的為人。我們可以先把媽媽分成兩大類：家庭主婦和職業婦女，然後分別形容她們的性格。

回答範例 1

Well, my mother is a traditional woman. She is a full-time housewife who takes care of everything in the family. She is hard-working, and she never complains about doing housework. She is an outgoing person, and she likes to make friends. I think she knows almost every single person in the building we live in. She gets emotional at times, and she cries when she watches Korean soap operas.

嗯，我的母親是個傳統婦女。她是一個全職的家庭主婦，她照料家裡的所有事情。她很勤勞，而且做家事從來不曾抱怨。她是個外向的人，喜歡交朋友。我覺得她幾乎認識我們住的大樓裡的每一個人。她有時候也會情緒化，而且她在看韓劇的時候還會哭。

回答範例 2

My mother is a career woman. She runs a business, and she has many people working under her. She devotes a lot of time to her business, but she never neglects us. Sometimes I wonder if she is a superwoman. I mean I wonder how she finds time to take care of me and my brother. She even has time to cook for us on weekends. Though her cooking skills are not the best, I appreciate what she did.

我的媽媽是個職業婦女。她經營公司，有很多人在她的管理下工作。她投入很多時間在她的公司上，但是她從不忽略我們。有時候我在想她是不是女超人。我的意思是，我不曉得她是如何找出時間照顧我和哥哥的。她在週末時甚至還有時間為我們煮飯。雖然她的廚藝不是最棒的，我很感謝她所做的。

重點補充

雖然媽媽都很偉大，不過人非聖賢。如果要說一說媽媽的壞話，也未嘗不可。

My mom is a talkative person. She can talk for hours. I always tell her to stop nagging at me. I am fifteen years old, but she talks to me as if I am five years old. I know that she cares about me. She is a kind person. She likes to chat with old people and help them. By the way, she is a good cook.

我的媽媽是個很愛講話的人。她可以講好幾個小時。我總是告訴她不要再對我嘮叨。我十五歲了，但是她跟我講話的方式好像我只有五歲而已。我知道她關心我。她是個善良的人。她喜歡和老人家聊天，並幫助他們。順便一提，她是個很棒的廚師。

9 Talk about a trip you took before. Where did you go? How was the trip?

談一談你去過的某一趟旅遊。你去了哪裡？那趟旅遊如何？

答題策略

這種詢問「有沒有出過國，去過什麼國家，最喜歡什麼國家」的問題，是口試常會問到的題目。建議先預設一個國家，到時候就能把答案套用在不同的題目。如果真的沒去過國外，也可以談談國內旅遊的經歷。

回答範例 1

I took a trip to Europe last year. I went to Switzerland. I have to say that it is the most beautiful country I have ever visited. The people there like to grow flowers, and you can see flowers of different colors. They are also very polite and helpful. I am also impressed by their culture. They like to keep the environment clean, and the trains are always on time.

去年我去了歐洲。我到了瑞士。我必須說，那是我所到過的最美麗的國家。那裡的人喜歡種花，你可以看到不同顏色的花。他們很有禮貌，也很熱心助人。他們的文化讓我印象深刻。他們喜歡保持環境乾淨，而且火車總是準時。

回答範例 2

I went to Kenting with my family last summer. It has been a long time since I went there. I felt so relaxed when I see the awesome scenery along the way. The sea was beautiful, and we did some water activities. I went diving and saw coral reefs with my own eyes for the first time. During the night, we visited the night market and also did some shopping. It was worth the trip.

去年夏天我和家人到墾丁去。距離上次去那裡已經過很久了。當我看到沿途的美景時，我覺得很放鬆。海很美，而我們也做了一些水上活動。我去潛水，並第一次親眼看到珊瑚礁。在晚上的時候，我們去了夜市，也買了一些東西。真是值得的旅程。

重點補充

不是每個人都有錢有閒，隨時都可以出國。如果你忙於課業或事業，根本沒時間出去玩的話，可以直接說明，然後把話題扯到日後最想要去的國家或地方。

I can't remember. It was too long ago. I am busy with my schoolwork/work so I have not been on a trip for a long time. After school/work, I am too tired to go anywhere. If I have the time and money, I would like to go to Japan. It's a beautiful country. I hope to go there when it snows. I love Japanese culture, so it will be great to visit Japan.

我不記得了。已經過太久了。我忙於課業（工作），以至於我已經很久沒去旅行了。放學（下班）後，我累得哪裡都不能去。如果我有時間和金錢的話，我想要去日本。日本是個美麗的國家。我希望在下雪的時候去。我很愛日本文化，所以去日本的話會很棒。

10 What's so great about the Internet? What do you usually do on the Net?

網路有什麼好處？你通常在網路上做什麼？

答題策略

網路的優點很多，平時用網路時，就是在利用網路的優點，所以也可以簡單交待在上網時所做的事情。如果平時很少上網，也說明原因，並針對其他人沉迷於網路提出一些看法。

回答範例 1

The best thing about the Internet is the information and services you can get for free. I enjoy reading articles about the things I am interested in. I also love YouTube because you can watch videos that are really funny. The Internet allows me to keep in touch with my friends with free services like Facebook and Gmail. I can't live without the Internet.

網路最棒的地方是可以免費得到的資訊和服務。我喜歡閱讀關於我感興趣事物的文章。我也喜歡 YouTube，因為你可以觀賞一些真的很好笑的影片。網路讓我用像是 Facebook 和 Gmail 的免費服務來和朋友保持聯絡。我不能沒有網路。

回答範例 2

I'm not really sure about that. I do not have Internet access at home because my mom thinks that I will spend too much time on it. I don't even have a smartphone. It's true that more and more people are addicted to the Internet. During lunch or dinner time, it is common to see people glued to their cell phones or tablets. My mom said that we should use the time to interact with people.

我不太確定。我在家裡沒有網路，因為媽媽認為我會花太多時間在網路上面。我甚至連智慧型手機也沒有。是真的有愈來愈多人沉迷於網路。在午餐和晚餐時間，人們緊緊盯著手機或平板是很常見的。我媽媽說我們應該利用那些時間來跟別人互動。

第 1 回
第 2 回
第 3 回
第 4 回
第 5 回
第 6 回

▶▶▶ 第三部分 看圖敘述

> 下面有一張圖片及四個相關的問題，請在 1 分半鐘內完成作答。作答時，請直接回答，不需將題號及題目唸出。
>
> 首先請利用 30 秒的時間看圖及問題。

提示
1. 照片裡的人在什麼地方？
2. 照片裡的人在做什麼？
3. 照片裡的人為什麼會在那裡？
4. 如果尚有時間，請詳細描述圖片中的景物。

1. 照片裡的人在什麼地方？停車場 car park / parking lot、巴士總站 bus terminal
2. 照片裡的人在做什麼、身邊有什麼？上巴士 get on the bus、行李 suitcase、把（行李）放到車上 lift onto the bus
3. 照片裡的人為什麼會在那裡？旅遊 travel、度假 on vacation
4. 如果尚有時間，請詳細描述圖片中的景物。年齡層 age group、人們的服裝 people's outfits

要取得高分，不能只說照片中看得到的東西，還必須針對看到的人、事和物做出聯想。以這張照片為例，可先點出最顯眼的事物，也就是巴士，再從巴士合理推斷照片拍攝的地點，即使無法判斷所在地，也能提出自己的猜想。地點交代完畢後，可以接著說一說照片中的人物，例如有幾個人站在什麼地方，年齡大約幾歲，可能是什麼關係，穿著打扮如何，正在做什麼，接下來可能會做什麼。最後可以加上從照片中得到的聯想，也就是敘述照片中沒有交代到的部分，還有自己的觀察與感想，例如圖中人物很明顯地是要參加搭巴士去旅遊，可以順便提到在台灣搭巴士旅遊的情況。

1. The first thing that caught my eye is...（第一個吸引我目光的是…）開頭的第一句可利用這個句型點出照片中的焦點，然後從這個點延伸出去。若不是用在第一句，可以改成 one thing that caught my eye is...（一個吸引我目光的事情是…）。

2. 由於無法百分之百確定照片拍攝的地點，對於照片中人物接下來會做什麼不太清楚，只是自己揣測，可以用到以下的表達：
我相信、認為 I believe、我認為 I think、我猜想 I guess、我認為 I suppose、我不曉得 I wonder、應該會 probably、可能 maybe、或許 perhaps。

3. 用 From what can be seen on the picture, ... 來表達從圖片中可以看到的細節，連接前面與後面所提到的重點。

回答範例

The first thing that caught my eye is the bus in the picture. I believe that the people waiting to get on the bus must have a certain place to go. I suppose they're either traveling somewhere on vacation. From what can be seen from the picture, these people look like they're in the twenties and in good spirits. There are at least six people in the picture and most of them have casual outfits like jeans or plaid shirts. The lady with a shoulder bag and sunglasses is stepping on the bus, while the bearded man standing behind her is carrying a backpack. Another girl in back of the man is adjusting the handle of her suitcase so that she can lift it onto the bus. Taking a bus is very common in Taiwan, partly because there are a quite a few out-of-town students and workers who leave or return to their homes by bus. It has become a part of their life.

範例中譯

這張照片中，第一個吸引我目光的是巴士；我相信這些等著上巴士的人，一定是要去某特定的地方。我想他們正要去旅行、度假。從照片可以看到的是，這些人看起來像二十歲左右而且精神很好。照片中至少有六個人，他們大部分都穿像牛仔褲或格子襯衫等休閒服裝。提著一個肩背包、戴太陽眼鏡的女子正準備上巴士；而站在她後面、有鬍子的男子，則拿著一個後背包；而在這位男子後面的另一個女子，正調整行李箱把手以便將它提上巴士。搭巴士在台灣很常見，部分原因是有不少學生、上班族會搭公車離鄉或返鄉，這已經成為他們生活的一部分了。

學習筆記欄

第四回　寫作能力測驗答題注意事項

1. 本測驗共有兩部分。第一部分為中譯英，第二部分為英文作文。測驗時間為 40 分鐘。

2. 請利用試題紙空白處背面擬稿，但正答務必書寫在「寫作能力測驗答案紙」上。在答案紙以外的地方作答，不予計分。

3. 第一部分中譯英請在答案紙第一頁作答，第二部分英文作文請在答案紙第二頁作答。

4. 作答時請勿隔行書寫，請注意字跡清晰可讀，並保持答案紙之清潔，以免影響評分。

5. 測驗時，不得在准考證或其他物品上抄題，亦不得有傳遞、夾帶小抄、左顧右盼或交談等違規行為。

6. 意圖或已經將試題紙攜出試場者，五年內不得報名參加本測驗。請人代考者，連同代考者，三年內不得報名參加本測驗。

7. 測驗結束時，須立即停止作答，在原位靜候監試人員收回全部試題紙及答案紙，清點無誤後，宣佈結束始可離場。

8. 應試者入場、出場及測驗中如有違反上列規則或不服監試人員之指示者，監試人員得取消應試資格並請其離場，且作答不予計分。

全民英語能力分級檢定測驗

中級寫作能力測驗

本測驗共有兩部份。第一部份為中譯英,第二部份為英文寫作。測驗時間為 40 分鐘。

一、中譯英 (40%)

說明:請將下列的一段中文翻譯成通順、達意且前後連貫的英文。

瑪莉買了兩張由五月天演唱的演唱會門票。她和男朋友迫不及待地想親眼目睹他們的偶像。雖然他們花了蠻多錢,但他們認為是值得的。瑪莉從來沒去過演唱會,所以她滿懷期待。她希望有機會和巨星們握手,並拿到他們的簽名。

二、英文作文 (60%)

請依下面所提供的文字提示寫一篇英文作文,長度約 120 字(8 至 12 個句子)。作文可以是一個完整的段落,也可以分段。(評分重點包括內容、組織、文法、用字遣詞、標點符號、大小寫。)

提示:飼養寵物可以為生活增添許多樂趣,不過同時也要負起某些責任。為什麼人們喜歡飼養寵物?你認為養寵物必須注意什麼?

第一部份請由第 1 行開始作答，請勿隔行書寫。　　　　　　　第 1 頁

5

10

15

20

25

30

35

40

第四回　口說能力測驗答題注意事項

1. 本測驗問題由耳機播放，回答則經麥克風錄下。分朗讀短文、回答問題與看圖敘述三部分，時間共約 15 分鐘，連同口試說明時間共需約五十分鐘。

2. 第一部份朗讀短文有 1 分鐘準備時間，此時請勿唸出聲音，待聽到「請開始朗讀」2 分鐘的朗讀時間開始時，再將短文唸出來。第二部分回答問題的題目將播出 2 遍，聽完第二次題目後要立即回答。第三部份看圖敘述有 30 秒的思考時間及 1 分 30 秒的答題時間，思考時不可在試題紙上作記號，亦不可出聲。等聽到指示開始回答時，請您針對圖片盡量的回答。

3. 錄音設備皆已事先完成設定，請勿觸動任何機件，以免影響錄音。測驗時請戴妥耳機，將麥克風調到嘴邊約三公分處，聽清楚說明，依指示以適中音量回答。

4. 評分人員將根據您錄下的回答（發音與語調、語法與字彙、可解度、及切題度等）作整體的評分。您可利用所附光碟自行測試，一一錄下回答後，再播出來聽聽，並斟酌調整。練習時請盡量以英語思考、應對，考試時較易有自然的表現。

5. 請注意測試時不可在試題紙上劃線、打「√」或作任何記號；不可在准考證或其他物品上抄題；亦不可有傳遞、夾帶小抄、左顧右盼或交談等違規行為。

6. 意圖或已將試題紙或試題影音資料攜出或傳送出試場者，視同侵犯本中心著作財產權，限五年內不得報名參加「全民英檢」測驗。請人代考，連同代考者，三年內不得報名參加本測驗。

7. 測驗結束時，須立即停止作答，在原位靜候監試人員收回全部試題紙且清點無誤後，等候監試人員宣布結束後始可離場。

8. 入場、出場及測驗中如有違反規則或不服監試人員指示者，監試人員將取消您的應試資格並請您離場，且作答不予計分，亦不退費。

全民英語能力分級檢定測驗

中級口說能力測驗

請在 15 秒內完成並唸出下列自我介紹的句子：

My seat number is（座位號碼後 5 碼），and my registration number is （考試號碼後 5 碼）.

第一部分：朗讀短文

請先利用 1 分鐘的時間閱讀下面的短文，然後在 2 分鐘內以正常的速度，清楚正確的讀出下面的短文，閱讀時請不要發出聲音。

Peter heard his friend mention an easy and quick way to make lots of money. Peter had always wanted to strike it rich but he wasn't fond of gambling. His friend persuaded him that it was an opportunity of a lifetime, and Peter would live to regret it if he missed it. Hence, Peter made up his mind to take a chance. In the end, the friend said the business failed and disappeared after that. Peter learned a painful lesson.

*　　　　　　　　*　　　　　　　　*

Many universities in Taiwan are feeling the impact of a low birthrate. With the decline of student population, universities that are less popular find it hard to attract outstanding students. There is no denying that there is an excess of universities. Some schools urged the government to allow students from China to receive education in Taiwan. The outcome remains to be seen.

第二部分：回答問題

這個部分共有 10 題。題目已事先錄音，每題經由耳機播出二次，不印在試卷上。第一至五題，每題回答時間 15 秒；第六至十題，每題回答時間 30 秒。每題播出後，請立即回答。回答時，不一定要用完整的句子，但請在作答時間內儘量的表達。

第三部分：看圖敘述

下面有一張圖片及四個相關的問題，請在一分半鐘內完成作答。作答時，請直接回答，不需將題號及題目唸出。

首先請利用 30 秒的時間看圖及問題。

提示：
1. 照片裡的人在什麼地方？
2. 照片裡的人在做什麼？
3. 照片裡的人為什麼會在那裡？
4. 如果尚有時間，請詳細描述圖片中的景物。

請將下列自我介紹的句子再唸一遍：

My seat number is（座位號碼後 5 碼）, and my registration number is（考試號碼後 5 碼）.

複試 寫作測驗 解析

▶▶▶ 第一部分 中譯英 (40%)

請將下列的一段中文翻譯成通順、達意且前後連貫的英文。

瑪莉買了兩張由五月天演唱的演唱會門票。她和男朋友迫不及待地想親眼目睹他們的偶像。雖然他們花了蠻多錢,但他們認為是值得的。瑪莉從來沒去過演唱會,所以她滿懷期待。她希望有機會和巨星們握手,並拿到他們的簽名。

翻譯範例

Mary bought two tickets to the concert which will be performed by MayDay. Her boyfriend and she can't wait to see their idols with their own eyes. Though they spent quite some money, they think it is worth it. Mary has never been to a concert, and she is full of anticipation. She hopes she has the opportunity to shake hands with the superstars and get their autographs.

逐句說明

1. 瑪莉買了兩張由五月天演唱的演唱會門票。

Mary bought two tickets to the concert which will be performed by MayDay.

　　這是一篇記敘文,翻譯的時候必須特別留意時態。雖然說明文通常用現在式,記敘文通常會用過去式,不過還是必須按照句意來判斷動作是否已經發生過了。「瑪莉買了兩張由五月天演唱的演唱會門票」這句話是標準的「S + V + O」句型,主詞 S 是「瑪莉」,動詞 V 是「買」,受詞 O 是「門票」。門票買了嗎?當然是買了,所以要用過去式。門票買了,不過 perform(演唱)這個動作還沒發生,所以要用未來式。「五月天演唱歌曲」,這是主動語態,英文的句構轉換成「歌曲將由五月天演唱」,是被動語態,要用 will be performed。

116

2. 她和男朋友迫不及待地想親眼目睹他們的偶像。

Her boyfriend and she can't wait to see their idols with their own eyes.

要提及主詞，但主詞超過一個人稱的情況下，英文的排序是「二→三→一」，第二人稱先寫，再寫第三人稱，第一人稱最後寫。例如「我和我的朋友」要寫成 My friend and I。這是英文展現君子風度的方式，先介紹你，再介紹他，自己放在最後。有些人會把 Her boyfriend and she 寫成 Her boyfriend and her，這個問題其實很容易解決。先把動詞找出來，放在動詞前的為主詞，用主格代名詞 she，放在動詞後的為受詞，用受詞代名詞 her。

Her boyfriend and she went to the party.（她和她的男友去了派對。）

I invited her boyfriend and her to the party.

（我邀請了她和她的男友去派對。）

「親眼目睹」就是 see something with one's own eyes（用自己的眼睛看到），而不是從電視轉播或在網路上看到。例如：I won't believe it until I see it with my own eyes.（直到我親眼看到為止，否則我是不會相信的。）「can't wait to V」是指「迫不急待去…」。例如：I can't wait to drive my new car.（我迫不及待要開我的新車。）

3. 雖然他們花了蠻多錢，但他們認為是值得的。

Though they spent quite some money, they think it is worth it.

英文的邏輯不同於中文，連接詞的功能是連接兩個句子，兩個句子由一個連接詞串連起來，不能用到兩個連接詞。這就是為什麼英文句子中「有 though（雖然）就沒 but（但是）」、「有 because（因為）就沒 so（所以）」的原因。若覺得有「雖然」卻沒有「但」很奇怪，可改用副詞 still（還是）。Though they spent quite some money, they still think it is worth it.（雖然他們花了蠻多錢，他們還是認為是值得的。）「他們認為是值得的」這句要用現在式，因為現在式的目的是強調現況。以現況而言，他們認為花蠻多錢買門票這件事是值得的。若用了過去式的 thought，則表示現在的想法和之前的不同。例如：I thought it was a great idea.（我以為那是個好點子。）這表示我現在的看法和之前的相反，不再認為那是個好點子了。

另外要注意拼字相似且容易搞混的單字，不要因拼字錯誤被扣分或讓人誤解文意，列舉如下：

though（雖然；儘管），thought（認為；想），through（穿越；透過），thorough（透徹的；詳細的）

4. 瑪莉從來沒去過演唱會，所以她滿懷期待。

Mary has never been to a concert, and she is full of anticipation.

現在完成式的 have been to 表示「已經去過某個地方」，have never been to 表示「從未去過某個地方」。連接詞 and 的用途很多，而連接兩個獨立的句子時，and 也可以代表「所以」的意思。例如：She lost her key, and she is looking for it.（她弄丟了鑰匙，所以她正在找。），要加上副詞變成 and so、and therefore 也可以。anticipation 和 expectation 的中文翻譯都是「期待」，在此短文的情境中，用 anticipation 比較適合。anticipation 是指很興奮的感覺，例如要打開禮物前的那種期待。expectation 則是指對他人的要求，期待他人有某種表現。例如：His parents have high expectations of him.（他的父母對他的期待很高。）He exceeded everyone's expectations.（他超越了大家的期待。）

5. 她希望有機會和巨星們握手，並拿到他們的簽名。

She hopes she has the opportunity to shake hands with the superstars and get their autographs.

know（知道）、think（認為）、believe（相信）、hope（希望）等動詞，後面可接名詞子句。例如 I know that（我知道某件事），I think that（我認為某件事情如何），I hope that（我希望怎樣）。that 在這裡可寫也可不寫。opportunity 和 chance 都是「機會」，不過 opportunity 比較正式，例如：This is an opportunity of a lifetime.（這是千載難逢的機會。）。autograph 和 signature 都是「簽名」，但是用法不同。偶像和作者的簽名要用 autograph，因為 autograph 是指名人、作家、音樂家的簽名，含有紀念價值，但刷卡後店員會說 Please sign here.（請在這裡簽名。），表示確認簽名，所以店員要的是我們的 signature，不是 autograph。

▶▶▶ 第二部分 **英文作文** (60%)

> 請依下面所提供的文字提示寫一篇英文作文，長度約 120 字（8 至 12 個句子）。作文可以是一個完整的段落，也可以分段。

 飼養寵物可以為生活增添許多樂趣，不過同時也要負起某些責任。為什麼人們喜歡飼養寵物？你認為養寵物必須注意什麼？

結構預設

根據提示，本文主要問了兩個問題：為什麼人們喜歡飼養寵物？養寵物必須注意什麼？飼養寵物最常見的原因就是為了作伴。在歐美國家，許多父母讓幼兒和寵物相處，除了給孩子作伴，還會培養孩子的責任感。養寵物必須注意的事項很多，但由於字數和時間的限制，不必一一列出。建議可選擇適用於一般大眾的要點來寫，例如寵物的種類、牠需要的空間及飼養寵物的費用。

草稿擬定

1. 喜愛寵物的人（pet lovers），同伴（companion），寂寞（loneliness）
2. 責任（responsibilities），三思而行（think twice），納入考量（take into consideration）
3. 更重要的是（More importantly），需遵守的義務和承諾（commitment）

作文範例

I believe most pet lovers ①treat their pets ②as part of the family. Dogs and cats are popular companions, and they help to cure loneliness. ③Keeping a pet is a great way to learn how to love and care for someone. ④However, ⑤pet ownership ⑥comes with certain responsibilities. ⑦Those who intend to keep a pet for the first time should ⑧think twice before they make a decision. There are several things to ⑨take into consideration, including the type of pet, the space it needs and the cost it takes to own one. ⑩More importantly, keeping a pet is a commitment that can take many years. ⑪To sum up, a pet is a living creature, not a toy or a product.

我相信大部分喜愛寵物的人，對待他們的寵物就像是對待家中的一分子。狗和貓是非常受歡迎的同伴，而且牠們有助於治療寂寞。飼養寵物是學習如何愛護和照顧他人的好方法。然而，飼養寵物伴隨著必要的責任。那些打算第一次飼養寵物的人，在做出決定前應該要三思而行。有幾件事必須納入考量，包括寵物的種類、牠需要的空間，以及飼養寵物所要支出的費用。更重要的是，飼養寵物是一個需要花很多年時間的義務和承諾。總之，寵物是有生命的生物，並不是玩具或產品。

重點文法分析

① treat 有「請客；治療；對待」三個完全不相同的意思，例如：Let me treat you to dinner.（讓我請你吃晚餐。）、The Chinese doctor treated my wound with herbal medicine.（那位中醫用草藥來治療我的傷口。）、I always treat the elderly with respect.（我總是尊敬地對待年長者。）

② as 做為介系詞主要表示「當作」，如中文的 treat their pets as part of the family（把他們的寵物當成家中的一分子來對待）同樣的用法有：see... as（把…看做…），view... as（視…為…），consider...（把…認定為…）。

③ 「V-ing is a great way to V」這個句型非常實用，可用來說明事物的優點，例如：Listening to English songs is a great way to learn English.（聽英文歌曲是學習英文的好方法。）

④ 前兩句提到人們養寵物的原因和好處，接著寫到養寵物的責任，就需要用轉折語 However 來表示語氣上的轉折，以表示養寵物要注意的地方。

⑤ 擁有寵物的主人為 pet owners，「寵物的所有權」為 pet ownership，「擁有房子」的名詞則是 home ownership。

⑥ comes with 可理解為「附帶，伴隨」，如文中 pet ownership comes with certain responsibilities（擁有寵物伴隨著必要的責任）。comes with 也可用在商品上，指某件商品「附贈」某些東西。The cell phone comes with a built-in camera, a pair of earphones, a battery and a battery charger.（這台手機附贈內建照相機、一副耳機、一顆電池還有電池充電器。）

⑦ Those people who 可省略為 Those who，因為省略掉的是 people，關係代名詞必須用 who。寫說明文的時候，建議主詞不要用第三人稱單數，例如 a person 或 anyone，主要是因為動詞得用我們比較不熟悉的第三人稱單數（主詞動詞要一致的原則）之外，還會牽扯到主詞性別的問題。請參考以

下主詞動詞一致原則的變化：

Those who intend to keep a pet for the first time should think twice before they make a decision.

Anyone who intends to keep a pet for the first time should think twice before he or she makes a decision.

⑧ 中文的「三思而行」，翻譯成英文變成 think twice（思考兩次）。

⑨ consider 是「考慮」，consideration 是「必須考慮的因素」，take into consideration 是「把…因素納入考量」。文中提出的考量因素有三個：the type of pet（寵物的種類），the space it needs（牠需要的空間），the cost it takes to own one（擁有寵物所要支出的費用）。

⑩ 文中提到的考量因素其實有第四點，「飼養寵物是一種需要長時間投入的義務」，這點比之前提到的三點更為重要，因此可以在下一句的句首，用 More importantly（更重要的是）加強語氣。

⑪ 雖然是 120 字左右的短文，還是可以利用一句話做為結語。結語可以用 To sum up（總之）來開頭，然後提出一些建議。

複試 口說測驗 解析

請先利用 1 分鐘的時間閱讀下面的短文，然後在 2 分鐘內以正常的速度，清楚正確的讀出下面的短文。

短文

Peter heard his friend mention an easy and quick way to make lots of money. Peter had always wanted to strike it rich but he wasn't fond of gambling. His friend persuaded him that it was an opportunity of a lifetime, and Peter would live to regret it if he missed it. Hence, Peter made up his mind to take a chance. In the end, the friend said the business failed and disappeared after that. Peter learned a painful lesson.

      *   *   *

Many universities in Taiwan are feeling the impact of a low birthrate. With the decline of student population, universities that are less popular find it hard to attract outstanding students. There is no denying that there is an excess of universities. Some schools urged the government to allow students from China to receive education in Taiwan. The outcome remains to be seen.

中譯

Peter 聽他朋友提到一個輕鬆又能快速賺大錢的方法。Peter 一直以來都想迅速致富，但他不喜歡賭博。他的朋友說服他說這是一生千載難逢的機會，如果 Peter 錯過的話一定會終身遺憾。因此，Peter 拿定主意要冒險一次。最後，他的這位朋友說生意失敗，在那之後就消失了。Peter 學到了一個慘痛的教訓。

　　　　　*　　　　　　　　*　　　　　　　　*

許多在台灣的大學正感受到低出生率的衝擊。隨著學生的人口下降，比較不受歡迎的大學發現很難去吸引傑出的學生。大學過剩是無可否認的事實。有些學校呼籲政府允許中國的學生來台接受教育。這樣的結果依然有待觀察。

高分解析

1 重要單字：mention [ˋmɛnʃən] 提到；strike it rich 獲得大量的金錢；fond [fɑnd] 喜歡的；gambling [ˋgæmblɪŋ] 賭博；persuade [pəˋswed] 說服；opportunity [ˏɑpəˋtjunətɪ] 機會；regret [rɪˋgrɛt] 後悔；hence [hɛns] 因此；fail [fel] 失敗；disappear [ˏdɪsəˋpɪr] 消失；university [ˏjunəˋvɝsətɪ] 大學；impact [ˋɪmpækt] 衝擊，影響；birthrate [ˋbɝθˏret] 出生率；decline [dɪˋklaɪn] 下降；population [ˏpɑpjəˋleʃən] 人口；popular [ˋpɑpjələ] 受歡迎的；attract [əˋtrækt] 吸引；outstanding [ˋaʊtˋstændɪŋ] 傑出的；deny [dɪˋnaɪ] 否認；excess [ɪkˋsɛs] 過度，過剩；urge [ɝdʒ] 呼籲；government [ˋgʌvənmənt] 政府；receive [rɪˋsiv] 收到，接收；education [ˏɛdʒʊˋkeʃən] 教育；remain [rɪˋmen] 保持，仍是

2 多音節單字的重音是朗讀時需要注意的重點，因為只要重音放錯，就有可能造成對方聽不懂的狀況，例如 u·ni·ver·si·ty 五個音節的字，重音在第三音節 ver 的位置，美國課本或書籍會用 uniVERsity，標出重音的部分。另外，有些雙音節的單字可同時當作名詞或動詞使用，當名詞的時候，重音通常落在第一個音節，當動詞的時候，重音通常落在第二個音節。例如 record 當名詞（紀錄），重音在前，唸 REcord。當動詞時重音在後 reCORD。同樣的發音原則還有 project 和 research。如果唸錯重音，會讓人覺得這個字怪腔怪調的，尤其長音節單字的重音擺錯很容易被聽出來，所以必須正確記住單字的重音才行。

3 朗讀高分技巧

以下朗讀文章中有顏色的單字需要唸稍微大聲一點，讓語調有起伏。文章中有 | 的地方表示可以稍做停頓，讓語氣更加從容，更有自信。

Peter heard his friend mention | an easy and quick way | to make lots of money. | Peter had always wanted to strike it rich | but he wasn't fond of gambling. | His friend persuaded him | that it was an opportunity | of a lifetime | and Peter would live to regret it | if he missed it. | Hence, | Peter made up his mind | to take a chance. | In the end, | the friend said the business failed | and disappeared after that. Peter learned a painful lesson.

*　　　　　　　　　*　　　　　　　　　*

Many universities in Taiwan | are feeling the impact of a low birthrate. | With the decline of student population, universities that are less popular | find it hard | to attract outstanding students. | There is no denying | that there is an excess of universities. Some schools urged the government | to allow students from China | to receive education in Taiwan. | The outcome remains to be seen.

▶▶▶ 第二部分 回答問題

> 這個部分共有 10 題。題目已事先錄音,每題經由耳機播出二次,不印在試卷上。第 1 至 5 題,每題回答時間 15 秒;第 6 至 10 題,每題回答時間 30 秒。每題播出後,請立即回答。回答時,不一定要用完整的句子,但請在作答時間內儘量的表達。

1　What do you often complain about?

你經常會抱怨什麼?

答題策略

學生經常抱怨功課太多,大人則抱怨工作太累,這兩個話題都很好發揮。當然,你也可以當個聖人,說自己很少抱怨,凡事存好心、做好事、說好話。

第
1
回 第
2
回 第
3
回

第
5
回 第
6
回

回答範例 1

Well, let me see. I always complain about having too much homework to do and too little time to do it. It has something to do with the culture in Taiwan. Parents think that teachers who give a lot of homework are hard-working teachers. That's why students have a lot of homework.

嗯,我看看。我總是抱怨要做的功課太多,而做功課的時間太少。這跟台灣的文化有關係。父母認為,出很多功課的老師才是勤勞的老師。那就是為什麼學生有很多功課。

回答範例 2

I seldom complain about anything. I am satisfied with everything I have. My mom says I have to be grateful for what I have. We should stop complaining because complaining doesn't help.

我很少抱怨任何事情。我對於我所擁有的一切都很滿足。我媽媽說我必須感謝我所擁有的事物。我們應該停止抱怨,因為抱怨並沒有幫助。

重點補充

這類「你經常…嗎?」的問題,如果自己沒有親身經歷,又或者不知道該說什麼,可以預設一個「代打」的人物,並把話題轉移到那個人身上。

I seldom complain, but my mom always does. She complains when it is too hot, and she also complains when it is too cold. She always complains that things are getting more expensive.

我很少抱怨,但是我媽媽總是這樣。太熱的時候她會抱怨,太冷的時候她也會抱怨。而她總是抱怨東西越來越貴。

2 Do you feel jealous of other people at times? What makes you feel jealous?

你有時候會嫉妒別人嗎?什麼事情讓你感到嫉妒?

jealous（嫉妒）和 envious（羨慕）的意思不太一樣，jealous（嫉妒）的意思比較負面。若選擇回答是，可以具體說明，例如同學成績比你好，或別人薪水比你高。若你選擇回答從來不嫉妒別人，也要說明原因和想法。

回答範例1

This is tough. I guess I feel jealous at times. Some of my friends have better grades, but they don't study a lot. It's really unfair. I study very hard, but I can't get good grades. Maybe I should learn from them.

這有點難。我想我有時候會感到嫉妒吧。有些朋友成績比我好，但是他們並沒有很用功讀書。真的很不公平。我很用功讀書，但是我卻得不到好成績。或許我應該向他們學習。

回答範例2

I don't think so. I am always cheerful so I don't get jealous. I am happy with what I have in life. My teacher told me that jealousy is like a disease. If you get jealous of other people, you will be unhappy.

我不這麼認為。我一直是個開朗的人，所以我不嫉妒。我對於我生命中所擁有的一切都很滿意。我的老師告訴過我，嫉妒就像一種疾病。如果你嫉妒別人，你就會不開心。

重點補充

除了成績，也可以嫉妒別人的長相，並提出合理的原因，不過這樣比較像在說自己的缺點。

I am jealous of my cousin. She is tall and slim. She eats a lot but she never gets fat. I don't understand why.

我嫉妒我的表姐。她又高又苗條。她吃很多但是從來不會變胖。我不明白為什麼。

3　Did you ever borrow money from someone?
你曾經跟別人借過錢嗎？

答題策略

如果回答跟別人借過錢，內容中要提到對方是誰，借了多少錢，為什麼需要借錢，多久以後還錢，以及跟別人借錢的感受。當然，你也可以反過來說一直以來都是別人向你借錢，你從沒向別人借過。

回答範例1

Yes, I did. I borrowed some money from a friend because I left my wallet at home. I returned the money to her the next day. However, I think it's not a good habit.

我有借過。我跟一位朋友借了一些錢，因為我把錢包留在家裡。隔天我就把錢還給她了。然而，我覺得這是一個不好的習慣。

回答範例2

No, I never did. I think it is embarrassing. I usually have enough money so I don't need to borrow money from anyone. However, my friends like to borrow money from me, and they never return it to me.

不，我從來沒有。我認為這很丟臉。我通常都會有足夠的錢，所以我不需要向任何人借錢。不過，我的朋友喜歡跟我借錢，而且他們從來都不還錢。

重點補充

若你借不到錢，也可以提出來，例如：你想要買房子，卻沒有足夠的存款，你可以回答你很希望有人願意借錢給你。

No. Who will lend me money? I want to buy a house but it is so expensive. I don't think the bank will lend me money. My parents? Forget about it.

不。誰會借我錢？我想要買間房子，但是太貴了。我不認為銀行會借我錢。我的父母？還是算了吧。

127

When was the last time you visited the dentist?

你上次去看牙醫是什麼時候？

答題策略

大家應該都有過到牙醫診所的經驗，回答時，時間點並不重要，重要的是要提到你去牙醫診所的感受。順便一提，不一定只有牙痛才去看牙醫，也有可能只是每年的例行性檢查，都可以當作回答。

回答範例 1

I don't remember when but it was just a few months ago. I don't have a toothache. It was just a yearly check-up. The dentist said I did a good job, and my teeth are OK. Phew!

我不記得是何時去的，不過是幾個月前。我沒有牙痛。只是每年的檢查。牙醫說我做得很好，我的牙齒都沒問題。幸好！

回答範例 2

It was a long time ago. I always brush my teeth after meals. I take good care of my teeth. I think going to the dentist is a terrible experience so I try to avoid it.

那是很久以前的事了。我在用餐後一直都會刷牙。我都會好好照顧我的牙齒。我認為去看牙醫會是很恐怖的經歷，所以我盡量避免去看牙醫。

重點補充

如果真的要描述去看牙醫的恐怖經驗，盡量用你會的單字來形容。

I went there last week. I had a toothache, and it was so painful. The dentist told me there was a hole in my tooth. I stayed there for nearly an hour. What a horrible experience!

我上個星期才去過。我那時牙痛，而且痛得要命。那個牙醫告訴我，我的牙齒有一個洞。我在那裡待了將近一個小時。真是恐怖的經驗！

5 Will you be annoyed if your friend is late for an appointment?

如果你的朋友跟你約好卻遲到的話，你會生氣嗎？

答題策略

這題的回答要看你的時間觀念而定。你可以說守時很重要，守時是一種尊重別人的表現。你也可以說遲到一下子可以理解，因為有時候你自己也會遲到。

回答範例 1

Yes, I guess so. Being on time is really important. It shows that you respect the person you are going to meet. I am always early so I expect my friends to do the same.

應該會吧。準時是很重要的。這表示你重視你要去見的人。我總是提早到，所以我期望我的朋友也一樣會早到。

回答範例 2

No, I won't. I can understand that sometimes people are late because of certain reasons. I can use my cellphone when I am waiting so I don't get annoyed. Sometimes, I will also be late.

不，我不會。我可以理解人們有時候會因為某些原因而遲到。當我在等待的時候，我可以用我的手機，所以我不會生氣。有時候，我也會遲到。

重點補充

回答「會」或「不會」之後不知道要怎麼接下去的話，可以使用 once（有一次…），用曾經發生過的某件事情來回答。

Yes, I will. Once, one of my friends was supposed to meet me at one o'clock for lunch. In the end, he came at two thirty. The restaurant was closed by then. I was really angry with my friend.

會，我會。有一次，我的一位朋友原本應該一點鐘跟我見面吃午餐。最後，他兩點半才來。餐廳那個時候已經休息了。我當時真的很氣我的那位朋友。

Did you tell a lie before? Why did you do it?
你之前有說過謊嗎？你為什麼要這麼做？

答題策略

英文的謊言有分 white lie（白色謊言）和 black lie（黑色謊言）。白色謊言是指無傷大雅的善意謊言，黑色謊言則是惡意欺騙別人以獲得自身利益的謊言。回答時建議以白色謊言為例。

回答範例 1

Of course I did. One of my friends asked me if I liked her new hairstyle, and I said I did. It was a lie because I think she looked better with long hair. I told her a lie because I didn't want to hurt her feelings. Perhaps I will like her new hairstyle after I get used to it.

當然有。我的一位朋友問我喜不喜歡她的新髮型，我當時說喜歡。那是一個謊言，因為我認為她長頭髮比較好看。我當時向她說謊，因為我不想傷害她的感受。或許等我習慣之後，我會喜歡她的新髮型。

回答範例 2

I think I did but it was something unimportant. I try to be honest most of the time because honesty is the best policy. If you tell a lie, you have to remember it and sometimes tell another lie. I think that is tiring so I choose to tell the truth or keep quiet.

我認為我有說過，不過那是一件不是很重要的事。大部分的時候我盡量誠實以對，因為誠實是最好的策略。如果你說了謊，你必須記得這個謊，而且有時候還要多說另一個謊。我認為這樣很累，所以我選擇說實話，不然就保持沉默。

重點補充

還有情況是，有些人因為信仰宗教或是個人的因素，就連善意的謊言也不能說。如果是這樣，就只能照實這麼回答了。

I am a Christian so I can't lie. Lying is a bad habit, and I always tell the truth. The Bible says, 'Know the truth and the truth shall set you free.'

我是基督徒，所以我不能撒謊。説謊是一個壞習慣，所以我總是説實話。聖經裡提到：「知道真相，真相會讓你得到解放。」

7 What festival do you look forward to the most?
你最期待什麼節慶？

答題策略

華人的主要節慶有 Chinese New Year（農曆新年）、Dragon Boat Festival（端午節）、Mid-autumn Festival（中秋節）、Tombsweeping Day（清明節）和 Ghost Month（中元節）。歐美的主要節慶有 Easter Day（復活節）、Halloween（萬聖節）和 Christmas（聖誕節）。可以從以上這些節慶來發揮。

回答範例 1

Let me see. I look forward to Chinese New Year the most. We can enjoy a long break. I can see many of my relatives. We always play some card games and gamble with real money. It is not a lot of money but it is very exciting. We play for the fun of it. The winners usually give a treat. I also enjoy the big dinner we have as a family. I can't wait for it.

我想想。我最期待農曆新年。我們可以享受長假。我可以看到很多親戚。我們總是會玩一些紙牌遊戲，並用真的錢來賭博。並不是用很多錢來賭，但是很刺激。我們是為了好玩才玩的。贏家通常要請客。我也喜歡一家人這樣一起享用大餐。我迫不急待新年的到來。

回答範例 2

My favorite festival is Christmas. I always dream of a white Christmas. This year I will spend my Christmas in Japan. I hope it snows because I have never seen snow with my own eyes. My friends and I have a habit of exchanging gifts during Christmas. It is fun guessing what my friends will get for me. I also enjoy shopping for presents.

我最喜歡的節日是聖誕節。我總是夢想著一個白色聖誕。今年我會在日本度過聖誕節。我希望會下雪，因為我從來沒有親眼看過雪。在聖誕節時，我和朋友有交換禮物的習慣。去猜朋友會給我什麼禮物非常有趣。我也喜歡去買聖誕禮物。

重點補充

若你是有另一半的人，也別忘了還有情人節可以回答。

My favorite festival is Valentine's Day. My boyfriend always buys me flowers and a special present. Last year, he gave me a LV (Louis Vuitton) handbag. I wonder if he will give me a diamond ring this year. I'm sorry. I am getting too excited.

我最喜歡的節日是情人節。我的男朋友總是會買花還有一份特別的禮物給我。去年，他送我一個 LV 手提包。我不知道今年他是否會送我鑽戒。抱歉，我太過興奮了。

8 Talk about a skill you would like to learn. Why do you think it is important?

談談你想學的某一種技能。為什麼你認為這個技能很重要？

答題策略

技能可分為運動上和職場上所需要的一些能力，例如：游泳、騎腳踏車、開車、快速打字、電腦繪圖等。記得要提到學習這個技能對你有什麼幫助，你打算什麼時候開始學。

回答範例 1

I would like to learn how to swim. I think swimming is an important skill. If I were a good swimmer, I could save someone else's life one day. Other than that, swimming will allow me to enjoy being in the sea. I would also like to learn surfing and diving. I hope it is not too late to begin learning now. I think I will sign up for a swimming course this summer.

我想要學游泳。我認為游泳是一個重要的技能。如果我是個游泳好手，有一天我有可能救別人一命。除此之外，游泳能讓我享受在海裡的感覺。我也想學衝浪和潛水。我希望現在開始學還不算太晚。我想我這個夏天將會報名游泳課程。

回答範例 2

One skill I want to learn is digital designing. One of my friends is very good at creating logos and pictures with computer software. She works at home and makes a lot of extra pocket money for herself. I thought I could learn it by reading a book but it turned out that I was wrong. My friend suggested that I take a computer course or watch some videos on the Internet.

我想學的一項技能是數位設計。我有一個朋友很會用電腦軟體創作商標和圖片。她在家上班，而且為自己賺了很多額外的零用錢。我以為看書就可以學會，但是我錯了。我朋友建議我去上電腦課程或在網路上看一些影片。

重點補充

對學生來說，要想到工作上需要的技能是有點困難，因此也可以提到生活中需要的技能，像是學開車。

I think driving is an important skill. My dad can drive but my mom can't. Sometimes my dad is tired after driving for many hours. I hope I can learn to drive so I can help him. I will be able to drive my mom to the hospital if she is sick. That's why I think driving is an important skill.

我認為開車是重要的技能。我爸爸會開車，但是我媽媽不會。有時候我爸爸在開了好幾個小時的車之後會很累。我希望我可以學會開車，這樣我就能幫他開車。如果我媽媽生病的話，我還可以開車載她去醫院。這就是我認為開車是重要技能的原因。

9　What's the most exciting thing you did recently?
你最近做過最刺激的事情是什麼？

這類「你所做過最…的事情」的問題真的比較困難。除非事先準備好，否則回答時可能會腦袋一片空白。對於此問題最簡單的回答就是坐 roller-coaster（雲霄飛車），或者回答騎腳踏車環島旅行也不錯。

回答範例 1

The most exciting thing I did recently was riding the roller-coaster. During our school graduation tour, we went to Jianhushan, which is a famous theme park in Taiwan. I have always been afraid of heights, but my friends challenged me to take the roller-coaster ride. I closed my eyes for most of the ride, but it was still so exciting. My heart was beating very fast even after I got off it.

我最近做過最刺激的事情是玩雲霄飛車。在畢業旅行的時候，我們去了劍湖山，那是台灣一個著名的主題樂園。我一直以來都很怕高，但是我的朋友挑戰我，要我去坐雲霄飛車。坐的時候大部分時間我都閉著眼睛，但還是很刺激。就算我從雲霄飛車下來後，我的心臟還是跳得很快。

回答範例 2

The most exciting thing I did recently was play cards with my friends. We didn't gamble, and no money was involved. It was exciting because the loser had to sing in public. I won three games in a row until I lost. I sang a happy birthday song to my friend.

我最近做過最刺激的事情是跟朋友打牌。我們沒有賭博，所以沒有牽涉到金錢。之所以很刺激是因為輸的人要在大家面前唱歌。直到我輸之前，我連贏了三場。我唱了一首生日快樂歌給我朋友聽。

重點補充

如果你平常很少出門社交，做的最刺激的事情就是玩電腦遊戲，那也只能實話實說了。

Well, I guess I am a boring person. The most exciting thing to me is to play computer games. I am playing a game, which has 99 levels. I am at level 98 now, and it is really exciting. I can't wait to finish the last level.

嗯，我想我是個無趣的人。對我來說，最刺激的事情就是玩電腦遊戲。我正在玩一個有 99 個關卡的遊戲，我目前在第 98 關，這真的是很刺激。我迫不及待想要完成最後一關。

第 1 回
第 2 回
第 3 回
第 4 回
第 5 回
第 6 回

10 Do you think money is the most important thing in life? Why or why not?

你認為金錢是生命中最重要的東西嗎？為什麼是？為什麼不是？

答題策略

說到金錢，或許你會聯想到中文佳句：「錢財乃身外之物，生不帶來、死不帶去。」不過，請勿把此中文佳句直接逐字翻譯成英文，因為這樣外國人是聽不懂的。而從這個方向去思考可以提到，錢當然很重要，不過比錢更重要的還有家庭和健康。

回答範例 1

Money is important because in modern society, you can't live without it. However, I don't think money is the most important in life. Personally, my family is the most important. We love one another. The relationship we have is something we cannot buy with money. I don't think money alone can make people happy.

錢很重要，因為在現代的社會，沒有錢根本沒辦法生活。然而，我不認為錢是生命中最重要的東西。以我個人來說，我的家人是最重要的。我們都愛著彼此。我們所擁有的感情是我們用錢也買不到的。我不認為只有金錢就會讓人快樂。

回答範例 2

In my opinion, the most important thing in life is good health. Some people work very hard for money, putting in long hours and giving themselves a lot of stress. I mean what use is money if you don't have a healthy body? If you sacrifice your health for money, no amount of money is going to help you get back your health.

依我的看法，生命中最重要的東西是健康。有些人為了錢很努力地工作，投入很長的工作時間，並給自己很多壓力。我的意思是，如果你沒有健康的身體，錢又有什麼用處呢？如果你為了錢犧牲健康，多少錢也不能幫你買回健康。

重點補充

當然，你也可以說錢就是萬能的，有錢才是最重要的，才不會讓人看不起。畢竟這是考英文，而不是考倫理道德，不用回答很正面的觀點。

Yes, I think money is the most important thing. People look down on you, including your family and friends, if you don't have money. I want to make a lot of money so I can enjoy my life. I want to live in a big house and drive a sports car. I can help the poor only when I am rich.

是的，我認為錢是最重要的東西。如果你沒有錢，人們會看不起你，包括你的家人和朋友。我想要賺很多錢，這樣我才能享受人生。我想要住大房子，還要開超跑。只有在我有錢的時候，我才能幫助窮人。

▶▶▶ 第三部分 **看圖敘述**

下面有一張圖片及四個相關的問題,請在 1 分半鐘內完成作答。作答時,請直接回答,不需將題號及題目唸出。

首先請利用 30 秒的時間看圖及問題。

提示　1. 照片裡的人在什麼地方?
　　　2. 照片裡的人在做什麼?
　　　3. 照片裡的人為什麼會在那裡?
　　　4. 如果尚有時間,請詳細描述圖片中的景物。

草稿擬定

1. 照片裡的人在什麼地方?機場 airport、出境大廳 departure hall、等待區 waiting area、報到 check-in、海關 customs
2. 照片裡的人在做什麼?彼此面對面坐著 sit and face one another、聊天 chat、登機 board the plane
3. 照片裡的人為什麼會在那裡?去國外 go abroad、旅行 on a tour、去旅遊 take a trip
4. 如果尚有時間,請詳細描述圖片中的人事物。排椅 row chair、明亮的日光 bright sunlight、戴口罩 wear masks、流行病 pandemic

把重點放在 Where，說明照片拍攝的地方，並舉出照片中的細節以支持自己的看法。照片中人物太多，沒有明確的焦點人物（Who），這種情況下只需要說明這群人大概在做什麼，不需要一個一個地交代。這麼多人聚集在某個地方，一定有一些原因。試著把這些原因交代清楚，也可以提到這些人接下來可能會做的事。不過如果照片中看到的、自己聯想的都說了，可是還有一些時間的話，建議繼續「聊」下去，說說自己的感想，甚至是自己生活中跟照片有關的事。

必殺萬用句

1. It is pretty obvious that this picture was taken...
   （很明顯，這張照片是在…拍攝的。）
   若照片的拍攝地點一目了然，就不需要說 If I am not mistaken, this picture was taken...（如果我沒弄錯的話，這張照片是在…拍攝的）。
   不過機場這麼大，If I am not mistaken 這句倒是可用來表示「如果我沒弄錯的話，這些人在機場的…（什麼地方）」。

2. That is, ...（也就是說）也是連接前後句的表達，後面可以加上要介紹自己的觀點。

3. Besides, ... 或是 In addition, ... 等表達後面可以加上其他要補充的細節，讓前、後句可以更順暢地連接在一起。

4. 雖然口說測驗對於文法的要求比較寬鬆，不過若能用正確的文法和句型來陳述，有助於加強表達能力，同時讓考官留下良好印象。形容詞子句是英語母語人士說話時經常用到的文法句型，學文法的時候會覺得很複雜，不過其實並不困難。只要把原本的兩個句子合併在一起，把代名詞 it 換成關係代名詞 which 或 that 就可以了。

5. It is noted that, ...（值得注意的是，…）後面可以加上照片的特別之處，讓考官知道你注意到照片中很醒目的重點。

It is pretty obvious that this picture was taken in an airport. There are four people in the picture. If I am not mistaken, they are in the departure hall. That is, they must have completed their check-in, gone through the customs, and had their passports examined. Now they're on the row chairs waiting to get on a plane. I guess the four people might be friends because they're sitting near and facing one another. The woman on the right has a small backpack and is wearing a cap, while the other woman on the left has a messenger bag and a carry-on luggage. Besides, the time of their departure may be in some daytime around summer since they have T-shirts or thin jackets on, and I can see bright sunlight in the background. By the way, it is noted that all of them are wearing masks, which reminds me of the pandemic worldwide at present.

很明顯的是,這張照片是在機場拍攝的。照片中有四個人,如果我沒弄錯的話,他們在出境大廳。也就是說,他們一定已經完成報到手續、過了海關並查驗完護照了,目前他們坐在排椅上等候上飛機。我猜這四人可能是朋友,因為他們都坐在附近而且面向著彼此。右邊這位女子有個小背包及戴著鴨舌帽,而左邊這位女子則背一個側背包並拿著登機行李。此外,他們出發的時間可能是夏季的某個白天,因為他們是穿著 T 恤或薄夾克,而且我可以看到背景是明亮的日光。順帶一提,值得注意的是他們都戴上口罩,這也讓我想到目前的全球疫情。

第五回　寫作能力測驗答題注意事項

1. 本測驗共有兩部分。第一部分為中譯英，第二部分為英文作文。測驗時間為 40 分鐘。

2. 請利用試題紙空白處背面擬稿，但正答務必書寫在「寫作能力測驗答案紙」上。在答案紙以外的地方作答，不予計分。

3. 第一部分中譯英請在答案紙第一頁作答，第二部分英文作文請在答案紙第二頁作答。

4. 作答時請勿隔行書寫，請注意字跡清晰可讀，並保持答案紙之清潔，以免影響評分。

5. 測驗時，不得在准考證或其他物品上抄題，亦不得有傳遞、夾帶小抄、左顧右盼或交談等違規行為。

6. 意圖或已經將試題紙攜出試場者，五年內不得報名參加本測驗。請人代考者，連同代考者，三年內不得報名參加本測驗。

7. 測驗結束時，須立即停止作答，在原位靜候監試人員收回全部試題紙及答案紙，清點無誤後，宣佈結束始可離場。

8. 應試者入場、出場及測驗中如有違反上列規則或不服監試人員之指示者，監試人員得取消應試資格並請其離場，且作答不予計分。

全民英語能力分級檢定測驗

中級寫作能力測驗

本測驗共有兩部份。第一部份為中譯英，第二部份為英文寫作。測驗時間為 40 分鐘。

一、中譯英 (40%)

說明：請將下列的一段中文翻譯成通順、達意且前後連貫的英文。

我外婆在我國小畢業的時候送了我一支手機作為獎勵，那也是我的第一支手機。雖然它帶給我很多方便，但同時也讓我的成績每況愈下。我在國中時，曾經因為上課玩手機被導師沒收過好幾次，我爸媽知道後決定不再讓我使用手機。自從我唸高中後就比較少在用手機了，不過我的成績反而因此進步了。

二、英文作文 (60%)

請依下面所提供的文字提示寫一篇英文作文，長度約 120 字（8 至 12 個句子）。作文可以是一個完整的段落，也可以分段。（評分重點包括內容、組織、文法、用字遣詞、標點符號、大小寫。）

提示：這幾年在台灣越來越流行直播，你對直播看法為何？以此為題，寫一篇英文作文。

1. 敘述台灣目前的直播現象。
2. 表達你對直播現象的看法。

第一部份請由第 1 行開始作答，請勿隔行書寫。　　　　　　第 1 頁

5

10

15

20

25

30

35

40

第五回 口說能力測驗答題注意事項

1. 本測驗問題由耳機播放，回答則經麥克風錄下。分朗讀短文、回答問題與看圖敘述三部分，時間共約 15 分鐘，連同口試說明時間共需約五十分鐘。

2. 第一部份朗讀短文有 1 分鐘準備時間，此時請勿唸出聲音，待聽到「請開始朗讀」2 分鐘的朗讀時間開始時，再將短文唸出來。第二部分回答問題的題目將播出 2 遍，聽完第二次題目後要立即回答。第三部分看圖敘述有 30 秒的思考時間及 1 分 30 秒的答題時間，思考時不可在試題紙上作記號，亦不可出聲。等聽到指示開始回答時，請您針對圖片盡量的回答。

3. 錄音設備皆已事先完成設定，請勿觸動任何機件，以免影響錄音。測驗時請戴妥耳機，將麥克風調到嘴邊約三公分處，聽清楚說明，依指示以適中音量回答。

4. 評分人員將根據您錄下的回答（發音與語調、語法與字彙、可解度及切題度等）作整體的評分。您可利用所附光碟自行測試，一一錄下回答後，再播出來聽聽，並斟酌調整。練習時請盡量以英語思考、應對，考試時較易有自然的表現。

5. 請注意測試時不可在試題紙上劃線、打「√」或作任何記號；不可在准考證或其他物品上抄題；亦不可有傳遞、夾帶小抄、左顧右盼或交談等違規行為。

6. 意圖或已將試題紙或試題影音資料攜出或傳送出試場者，視同侵犯本中心著作財產權，限五年內不得報名參加「全民英檢」測驗。請人代考，連同代考者，三年內不得報名參加本測驗。

7. 測驗結束時，須立即停止作答，在原位靜候監試人員收回全部試題紙且清點無誤後，等候監試人員宣布結束後始可離場。

8. 入場、出場及測驗中如有違反規則或不服監試人員指示者，監試人員將取消您的應試資格並請您離場，且作答不予計分，亦不退費。

全民英語能力分級檢定測驗

中級口說能力測驗

請在 15 秒內完成並唸出下列自我介紹的句子：

My seat number is（座位號碼後 5 碼）, and my registration number is （考試號碼後 5 碼）.

第一部分：朗讀短文

　　請先利用一分鐘的時間閱讀下面的短文，然後在二分鐘內以正常的速度，清楚正確的讀出下面的短文，閱讀時請不要發出聲音。

　　English proverbs are the wisdom and experience of human lives. They have been passed down from generation to generation for centuries. To make proverbs easier to remember, a couple of key words in some sentences begin with the same consonant or end with the same vowel. Examples like "Practice makes perfect" and "No pains, no gains" are usually catchier and used more often than other expressions.

*　　　　　　　*　　　　　　　*

　　Generally, fortune cookies are believed to derive from the United States; however, they originated from Japan in reality. In the nineteenth century, similar cookies like pancakes were found in Japanese temples. Later in the early twentieth century, it is said that a Japanese immigrant brought such snacks to America for business. Whichever country fortune cookies are from, they have made their mark on Americans.

第二部分：回答問題

　　這個部分共有 10 題。題目已事先錄音，每題經由耳機播出二次，不印在試卷上。第一至五題，每題回答時間 15 秒；第六至十題，每題回答時間 30 秒。每題播出後，請立即回答。回答時，不一定要用完整的句子，但請在作答時間內儘量的表達。

第三部分：看圖敘述

　　下面有一張圖片及四個相關的問題，請在一分半鐘內完成作答。作答時，請直接回答，不需將題號及題目唸出。

　　首先請利用 30 秒的時間看圖及問題。

提示：
1. 照片裡的人在什麼地方？
2. 照片裡的人在做什麼？
3. 照片裡的人為什麼會在那裡？
4. 如果尚有時間，請詳細描述圖片中的景物。

請將下列自我介紹的句子再唸一遍：

My seat number is（座位號碼後 5 碼）, and my registration number is （考試號碼後 5 碼）.

複試 寫作測驗 解析

▶▶▶ 第一部分 中譯英 (40%)

請將下列的一段中文翻譯成通順、達意且前後連貫的英文。

我外婆在我國小畢業的時候送了我一支手機作為獎勵,那也是我的第一支手機。雖然它帶給我很多方便,但同時也讓我的成績每況愈下。我在國中時,曾經因為上課用手機玩遊戲被導師沒收過好幾次,我爸媽知道後決定不再讓我使用手機。自從我唸高中後就比較少在用手機了,不過我的成績反而因此進步了。

翻譯範例

My grandmother gave me a cell phone as a reward when I graduated from elementary school. That was also my first one. Although it brought much convenience to me, it made my grades go from bad to worse at the same time. When I was in junior high school, my homeroom teacher took away my cell phone several times because I played games on it in class. My parents decided not to let me use the cell phone after they knew it. I have used my cell phone less often since I studied in senior high school; however, my grades are getting better instead.

逐句說明

1. 我外婆在我國小畢業的時候送了我一支手機作為獎勵,那也是我的第一支手機。

   My grandmother gave me a cell phone as a reward when I graduated from elementary school. That was also my first one.

「作為獎勵；回報」的英文句型為「as a reward」，後面可以加上「for + doing sth/N」，例如：He gave his daughter a laptop as a reward for her hardworking.（他送他的女兒一台筆電當作她努力的獎勵。）英文也有一句諺語是 Virtue is its own rewards.（善行本身就是回報。）

2. 雖然它帶給我很多方便，但同時也讓我的成績每況愈下。

Although it brought much convenience to me, it made my grades go from bad to worse at the same time.

　　這句可以直接用直譯來表達，然而因為句中有出現一個成語「每況愈下」，在考試時看到這個成語可能會愣住，不知如何下筆。然而「每況愈下」在英文中也有相似的表達，也就是「go from bad to worse」，例如：Things have gone from bad to worse.（事情已經每況愈下。）

3. 我在國中時，曾經因為上課用手機玩遊戲被導師沒收過好幾次，我爸媽知道後決定不再讓我使用手機。

When I was in junior high school, my homeroom teacher took away my cell phone several times because I played games on it in class. My parents decided not to let me use the cell phone after they knew it.

　　導師的英文是「homeroom teacher」，而「沒收」這個詞的英文可以用片語「take away」來表達。用手機玩遊戲的英文則是「play games on the phone」，而在翻譯中因為前面有提到 cell phone 這個單字，所以會以代名詞 it 來代替。

4. 自從我唸高中後就比較少在用手機了，不過我的成績反而因此進步了。

I have used my cell phone less often since I studied in senior high school; however, my grades are getting better instead.

　　「比較少」這種頻率副詞可以用「rarely」或是「less often」來表達，而「自從…」則是要用「since」來連接。另外要注意的是「however」不能直接連接兩個句子，因此要在 however 前面加上分號「;」才可以連接兩個句子。「反而」在英文中要用「instead」來表達，並且放在句尾。

▶▶▶ 第二部分 **英文作文**（60%）

> 請依下面所提供的文字提示寫一篇英文作文，長度約 120 字（8 至 12 個句子）。作文可以是一個完整的段落，也可以分段。

提示 這幾年在台灣越來越流行直播，你對直播看法為何？請敘述台灣目前的直播現象，並表達你對直播現象的看法，以此為題，寫一篇英文作文。

結構預設

本題要求考生寫出台灣目前流行的直播現象，包括在台灣做直播的模式、直播會流行的原因等，以及考生對直播的看法，可以提出你支持直播，或是不支持直播，並且提出其中的原因，例如：直播可以讓人們認識不一樣的人事物，或是直播帶來的負面影響等，都可以在寫作中發揮出來。

草稿擬定

1. 在台灣的直播平台（live stream platform）增加，許多人開始主持（host）直播節目。直接開門見山，以 With the increase of live stream platforms, many people in Taiwan start hosting live streams on the Internet.（隨著直播平台的增加，台灣許多人開始在網路上主持直播。）

2. 說明台灣主持直播節目的人會做什麼活動，例如：評論時事（comment about current events）、展現才藝（show their talents）、販賣商品（sell products）等。

3. 主持直播節目的人（live streamer），他們著重的點可能是影片的觀看數（views）、或是名聲（fame and popularity）、市場背後的商業機會（business opportunities behind the market）等。

4. 最後提到自己對台灣直播文化的想法，並談談自己認為人們在直播文化所扮演的角色。

①With the increase of live stream platforms, many people in Taiwan start hosting live streams on the Internet. They interact with the audiences ②by commenting about current events, showing their talents, and selling products and everything in between. Some live streamers become famous or even ③make a lot of money out of hosting live stream shows. Views about live streaming ④differ from person to person. Some pursue the fame and popularity of being online celebrities while others see the great business opportunities behind the market. ⑤To my way of thinking, it is just another form of interpersonal communication, so there is no need to ⑥make a fuss over it. Whatever our role is on live stream platforms, we should always protect ourselves, respect others, and avoid Internet addiction.

隨著直播平台的增加,台灣許多人開始在網路上主持直播。他們透過評論時事、表演才藝、販賣商品等任何事來跟觀眾互動。有些直播主因為主持節目而成名或甚至賺了不少錢。對直播的看法大家見仁見智。有些人追求成為網路紅人帶來的名聲與人氣,有些人則看到了這市場背後的龐大商機。我的看法是,這只是人際溝通的另一種形式,所以並不需要大驚小怪。不管我們在直播平台中是扮演什麼角色,我們應該總是保護自己、尊重他人,及避免網路成癮。

① 介紹某個現象發生的情形，可以用開門見山、破題的方法來寫作，「隨著直播平台的增加…」With the increase of live stream platforms, ... 介系詞 With 有很多意思，在這裡則是「隨著…」的意思。

② 「藉由、透過」可以用「by」來表示，後面加上名詞或動名詞，因此寫作可以寫成 by commenting about current events...

③ make a lot of money out of V-ing（活動）指的是透過做某個活動來賺很多錢，因此要表達透過主持直播節目來賺錢，則可以寫成 make a lot of money out of hosting live stream shows。

④ differ from person to person 指的是每個人的看法都不同，意思近似於中文的成語「見仁見智、因人而異」。

⑤ 要表達自己的想法，可以用 To my way of thinking, ... 來表達，意思是「照我的想法來看」。

⑥ 若要表達對某個人事物太過關注、小題大作，在英文可以用 make a fuss over it 來表達。

複試 口說測驗 解析

第
1
回
第
2
回
第
3
回
第
4
回
第
5
回
第
6
回

▶▶▶ 第一部分 朗讀短文

> 請先利用 1 分鐘的時間閱讀下面的短文，然後在 2 分鐘內以正常的速度，清楚正確的讀出下面的短文。

短文

English proverbs are the wisdom and experience of human lives. They have been passed down from generation to generation for centuries. To make proverbs easier to remember, a couple of key words in some sentences begin with the same consonant or end with the same vowel. Examples like "Practice makes perfect" and "No pains, no gains" are usually catchier and used more often than other expressions.

　　　　＊　　　　　　　　＊　　　　　　　　＊

Generally, fortune cookies are believed to derive from the United States; however, they originated from Japan in reality. In the nineteenth century, similar cookies like pancakes were found in Japanese temples. Later in the early twentieth century, it is said that a Japanese immigrant brought such snacks to America for business. Whichever country fortune cookies are from, they have made their mark on Americans.

中譯

英文諺語是人類生活的智慧與經驗，這些諺語已經代代相傳了好幾世紀。為了讓諺語更容易，有些句子的幾個關鍵詞用同樣的子音開頭，或用同樣的母音結尾。比方說，「熟能生巧」（子音 p）及「一分耕耘，一分收獲」（母音

ai）通常比其他句子更好記且更常用。

*　　　　　　　*　　　　　　　*

一般來說，大家都相信幸運餅乾來自美國；但其實它們起源於日本。在十九世紀，類似像薄煎餅的餅乾出現在日本寺廟。之後在二十世紀初，據說有位日本移民把這樣的點心帶到美國去做生意。不管幸運餅乾來自於哪個國家，它們已經在美國人心中留下深刻的印象了。

高分解析

1 重要單字：proverb ['pravɜb] 諺語；wisdom ['wɪzdəm] 智慧；pass down 傳下來；generation [ˌdʒɛnə'reʃən] 世代；consonant ['kɑnsənənt] 子音；vowel ['vauel] 母音；catchy ['kætʃɪ] 易記的；expression [ɪk'sprɛʃən] 表達；generally ['dʒɛnərəlɪ] 通常；fortune ['fɔrtʃən] 好運；originate [ə'rɪdʒəˌnet] 來自；immigrant ['ɪməgrənt]（外來）移民

2 第一篇短文提到有些諺語的開頭會用同樣的子音、結尾用同樣的母音。例如，"Practice makes perfect" 這句都是用同樣的子音 p；而 "No pains, no gains" 這句都是用 no 開頭，而下個單字都是由母音 ai 組成的，在發音上可以注意這些諺語的押韻。

3 朗讀高分技巧

以下朗讀文章中有顏色的單字需要唸稍微大聲一點，讓語調有起伏。文章中有 | 的地方表示可以稍做停頓，讓語氣更加從容，更有自信。

English proverbs are the wisdom and experience of human lives. | They have been passed down from generation to generation for centuries. | To make proverbs easier to remember, | a couple of key words in some sentences begin with the same consonant | or end with the same vowel. | Examples like "Practice makes perfect" | and "No pains, no gains" | are usually catchier and used more often than other expressions.

　　　*　　　　　　　*　　　　　　　*

Generally, | fortune cookies are believed to derive from the United States; | however, | they originated from Japan in reality. | In the nineteenth century, | similar cookies like pancakes | were found in Japanese temples. | Later in the early twentieth century, | it is said that a Japanese immigrant | brought such snacks | to America for business. | Whichever country fortune cookies are from, | they have made their mark on Americans.

▶▶▶ 第二部分 回答問題

> 這個部分共有 10 題。題目已事先錄音，每題經由耳機播出二次，不印在試卷上。第 1 至 5 題，每題回答時間 15 秒；第 6 至 10 題，每題回答時間 30 秒。每題播出後，請立即回答。回答時，不一定要用完整的句子，但請在作答時間內儘量的表達。

1 Do you like to work out at a gym or at home? Please explain.

你比較喜歡到健身房運動還是在家運動？請解釋原因。

答題策略

回答這題需要先選出傾向在健身房運動或是在家裡運動，如果喜歡在健身房運動，則要提出喜歡的原因，像是健身房提供很多運動器材（fitness equipment）可以選擇，或是有健身教練（fitness coach）可以協助你等等。而喜歡在家運動則要說明其中的原因，或是在家運動與在健身房運動之間的不同。

I like to work out at a gym because there are many pieces of fitness equipment to choose from, and fitness coaches are always there for me if I need help at the gym. Above all, working out with fitness partners makes me more energetic and motivated.

我喜歡到健身房運動。因為有很多運動器材可以選擇,而且我如果在健身房需要協助,隨時都可以找到健身教練。最重要的是,跟運動夥伴一起健身讓我更有精神及動力。

I prefer to work out at home. The main reason is that it costs a lot of money to get a gym membership since I'm still a student. Besides, using simple tools to work out such as push-ups or sit-ups can also reach the same goal. For me, I just want to look fit, not muscular.

我比較偏好在家運動。主要的原因是加入健身房的會員很花錢,而且我目前還是學生。另外,使用簡單器具做像是伏地挺身或仰臥起坐等運動,也可以達到一樣的目標。對我來說,我只想看起來勻稱,而不是壯碩。

重點補充

這類題目不是議論文,因此不需要提出明確的立場。如果你在健身房和家裡都能夠運動,你可以用以下的敘述來回答。

It's hard to say. It depends. If I have enough money and want to be muscular, I will go to the gym. On the other hand, if I want to save money, I will work out at home.

這很難說,要看情況。如果我有足夠的錢,而且想要變更壯,我會去健身房。另一方面,如果我想要省錢,我就會在家運動。

你最喜歡什麼類型的電影？

第 1 回
第 2 回
第 3 回
第 4 回
第 5 回
第 6 回

答題策略

回答這個問題前要知道電影類型的英文，例如：動作（Action）、科幻（science fiction）、喜劇（Comedy）、戲劇（Drama）、奇幻（Fantasy）、恐怖（Horror）、浪漫（Romance）等，並從中挑選出自己喜歡的電影類型並說明原因，也可以舉例這個類型有哪些電影。

回答範例 1

I'm a huge fan of science fiction. I've been fascinated by stores about space or robots since I was little. Watching movies like *Star Wars* series or *Avatar* can expand my imagination, and their special effects really take my breath away.

我是科幻片的頭號粉絲。我從小就對有關太空或機器人的故事非常著迷。觀賞像《星際大戰》系列或《阿凡達》等電影可以開拓我的想像力，而且它們的特效真的讓我嘆為觀止。

回答範例 2

My favorite type of movie is drama films. Some of them are based on true events while some others are from best-selling novels. These movies are mostly inspirational and touching. I've always believed that drama movies can reflect the reality of the world and human nature.

我最喜歡的電影類型是劇情電影。這些電影有的是根據真實事件，有的則是來自暢銷小說。這些電影大多鼓舞人心又很感人。我一直相信劇情片可以反映世界及人性的真實面。

Do you believe in ghosts or aliens? Why?
你相信鬼魂還是外星人的存在？為什麼？

答題策略

這題總共有兩個問題，首先要回答你相信鬼魂還是外星人的存在，再者，不論你相信哪一種，都要說明原因。另外，如果你認為這兩者都不存在，也要說明為什麼不相信，才能回答出完整的論述。

回答範例 1

Personally, I think I believe in ghosts. Part of the reason is that I was born to have "yin-yang eyes," so I'm more sensitive to paranormal events than others. Also, there was one time when I saw the soul of my best friend in person after his death. Therefore, I believe that ghosts do exist.

就我個人而言，我覺得我相信鬼魂的存在。部分原因是我生來就有「陰陽眼」，所以我對超自然事件會比其他人還敏感。而且，我有一次曾經親眼見到我摯友過世後的靈魂，因此我相信鬼魂的確存在。

回答範例 2

I'm not sure about that, but I guess I'm more of a believer in aliens. While most photos of the spirits or haunted houses might have been photoshopped, there are more and more news reports about the sightings of aliens or creatures from outer space. So I'd rather believe in the latter.

我不太確定，不過我猜我應該比較相信有外星人。大多數關於幽靈或鬼屋的照片也許有經過修圖，而有關目擊外星人或外太空生物的新聞報導則越來越多。所以我寧可相信後者。

如果你不信鬼魂，也不相信外星人，可以回答你兩者都不相信，並說明其中的原因。

Honestly, I have no idea. I don't believe in either ghosts or aliens. I've never seen any of them. I also think that all the stories about ghosts and aliens are fake. Those stories are made up by people's fear.

老實說，我不知道。我不相信鬼魂或外星人的存在，我從來沒有見過任何一個鬼魂或外星人。我也認為所有關於鬼魂和外星人的故事都是假的，這些故事是由人們的恐懼所編造出來的。

4 Have you ever cheated on an exam? Why or why not?

你曾在考試中作弊嗎？為什麼有或為什麼沒有？

答題策略

這題總共問了兩個問題，考生可以依照自己的經驗來回答，若之前有作弊過，也是可以提出來，並且說明作弊的原因，只要回答出合理的論述，都會拿到分數。若是沒有作弊過，也要說明為什麼你沒有這麼做，讓整個敘述更完整。

回答範例 1

I admit that I cheated on a test once. I remember it was chemistry, my weakest subject. I copied the formulas from a note I wrote earlier. Later, I got caught on the spot and failed the course. I did this because I wasn't interested in chemistry, but I know it served me right.

我承認我曾經在一次的考試作弊。我記得那是化學，我最弱的科目。我將之前在紙條上寫的公式抄在考卷上。後來，我當場被抓到，而這門課也被當了。我這麼做是因為我對化學根本沒興趣，但我知道是我自己活該。

As a student, "cheat" isn't in my dictionary. I know students hope to have good grades, but I can't see why some of them would stop at nothing for what they want. I would rather be defeated in a fair play than get number one in a foul play. So cheating is the last thing I would do on an exam.

身為學生，我的字典中絕沒有「作弊」這個詞。我知道學生都希望有好成績，但我不明白為什麼有些人會不擇手段得到他們想要的。我寧可在公平競爭中被打敗，也不要以犯規中得第一。所以我在考試中絕不可能會作弊。

5 What are your pet peeves? Tell us about your experience.

有什麼會讓你抓狂的事情？告訴我們你的經驗。

答題策略

首先，題目中提到 pet peeve，若不知道這個詞是指「最討厭的事情」，就可能會回答成跟寵物相關的話題，這樣反而會得不到分數。要回答這題，首先要講出自己最受不了的事情是什麼，並說明自己之前的經驗。回答範例 1 中提到 push one's buttons 這個片語，意思是「使某人生氣」。

回答範例 1

I have a pet peeve about people using cell phones at a meeting or a movie theater. It's annoying and can drive me crazy. If I were there, I would directly ask the person to switch off the cell phone or to use it outside. My friends say I'm easy-going, but those using cell phones in the wrong places really push my buttons.

我無法忍受有人在會議或電影院中使用手機。這很令人討厭，而且會讓我抓狂。如果我在現場的話，我會直接請對方把手機關機，或請他到外面使用手機。我朋友說我很隨和，但那些在不當的場合使用手機的人，真的會踩到我的地雷。

回答範例 2

There are many things I can't stand, and my biggest pet peeve is when someone cuts in line. Getting in line is considered basic manners in many cultures; those jumping in the queue are simply asking for trouble. Some people might tolerate this behavior, but I'm definitely not one of them.

我有很多事情無法忍受,而最讓我最不高興的就是別人插隊。排隊在許多文化中被視為基本禮貌,至於那些插隊的人簡直是自找麻煩。有些人可能會容忍這樣的行為,但我絕對不會是其中一位。

重點補充

如果你是胸襟闊、度量大的好好先生、小姐,你可能很少有讓你不高興的事情,沒有所謂的不愉快經驗。這樣的話可以先說明自己沒有生氣的經驗,把話題轉過來,談一談愉快的經驗。

I can't think of any. I seldom get mad at something. When I am with my friends, they always respect me. They smile and treat me politely. I hope I will never be angry at something. Having a bad temper is not a good thing.

我想不出任何事情。我很少為某件事生氣。當我和我的朋友在一起時,他們總是尊重我。他們微笑並有禮貌地對待我。我希望我永遠不會為某件事生氣。脾氣不好並不是什麼好事。

---

6 Should teenagers be allowed to use credit cards? Why or why not?

青少年應該被允許用信用卡嗎?為什麼或為什麼不?

答題策略

這題包含了兩個問題,在回答時要提到青少年應不應該使用信用卡,並且說明你為什麼會這樣認為。回答時可能會用到的英文詞彙有小額付款(micropayment)、金融卡(debit card)、理財的(financial)、刷爆信用卡(max out credit card)等。

Why not? I think teenagers have the right to make use of their money and choose their payment like adults. While most of their parents use credit cards, teenagers can have additional cards for micropayment or debit cards, which take money directly from their bank accounts. In addition, parents can take this opportunity to teach their children financial skills through using credit cards.

有何不可？我覺得青少年有權利跟成年人一樣使用金錢及選擇付款方式。由於他們的家長多半會使用信用卡，青少年可以辦為了小額付款的附卡，或是簽帳金融卡，直接從銀行帳戶中扣款。此外，家長可以藉此機會教孩子透過使用信用卡了解理財技巧。

I don't think it's the right time for teenagers to have credit cards. If they have one, there might be the consequences of spending too much on unnecessary things or even maxing it out. In the end, it's always their parents who have to clean up the mess. Teenagers are still too young to be independent financially, so I suggest they be allowed to use credit cards only when they have a job.

我認為青少年使用信用卡還不是時候。如果他們有信用卡，就可能造成花太多錢在不必要的事情上，甚至將卡刷爆的後果；最後還是要由他們爸媽來收拾殘局。青少年的年紀還太小，沒辦法經濟獨立；因此我建議等他們有工作時，再使用信用卡。

7 If you had a chance to write an e-mail to the President, what would you say to him/her?

如果你有機會寫電子郵件給總統，你會跟他／她說什麼？

答題策略

這題的回答會需要更多思考時間，你可以提到你希望總統關心的議題，因此回答時可能會用到許多與社會議題相關的詞彙，例如：天災（natural disaster）、治安（safety issue）、教育政策（educational policy）、社會資源

（social resource）等，回答時用這些詞彙會讓敘述更加豐富。

回答範例 1

Dear Mr. President, I hope this email finds you well. Thank you for working so hard to make our country a better place to live. We know there are many things you have to take care of these years, including natural disasters, safety issues, educational policies, and so on. You always give pep talks on TV and tell us to have faith in our country. Likewise, we expect you can keep the promises you made.

親愛的總統先生，希望您收到這封信時一切安好。感謝您這麼努力，讓我們國家成為更好的居住環境。我們知道您在這幾年有很多事情要處理，包括天災、治安問題、教育政策等等。您總是在電視上精神喊話，告訴我們要對國家有信心；同樣地，我們也期待您可以履行您之前答應過的諾言。

回答範例 2

Dear Ms. President, how have you been? I'm a sophomore in senior high school. Over the years, the gap between the rich and the poor has remained a problem in our country. While wealthy people have plenty of social resources, those living in poverty like us can hardly get by on low incomes. I suggest you come up with a better tax policy. I wish your team could see it in our way. Thank you.

親愛的總統女士，您好嗎？我是一名高二生。這幾年來，貧富差距仍是國內的一項問題。有錢人擁有不少社會資源，而像我們生活貧困的人則幾乎無法靠微薄收入來維生。我建議您應該想出更好的賦稅政策，希望您的團隊能考量我們的立場。感謝您。

8 **Are you a dog person or a cat person? Please give examples.**

你是愛狗的人還是愛貓的人？請舉例說明。

第1回
第2回
第3回
第4回
第5回
第6回

這題比較容易回答，題目中提到的 dog person、cat person，指的是「愛狗的人」和「愛貓的人」，因此回答需要提到自己比較喜歡狗，或是比較喜歡貓，並舉例說明喜歡這些動物的原因。

回答範例 1

Dogs and cats are both adorable pets, but if I have to choose one between the two, it would be the former. Dogs are smart, playful, and faithful to their owners. They are naughty at times, but they're also trainable. I've had a male Labrador for five years. He's very clingy with my family and isn't afraid of strangers. Sometimes he looks as if he knows what I'm thinking. That's why I love dogs more than cats.

狗跟貓都是可愛的寵物，但如果非要二選一的話，我會選前者。狗很聰明、愛玩、而且對主人忠心。牠們有時候很調皮，但牠們可以被訓練。我養一隻公的拉布拉多狗有五年了，他很黏我的家人，而且不怕陌生人。有時候他看起來似乎知道我在想什麼，這也是我愛狗勝過貓的原因。

回答範例 2

To my mind, I prefer cats to dogs. Although I can't deny that I have more friends with dogs than those who keep cats, there are some traits found in cats instead of dogs indeed. From my friends' experience, taking care of cats is a lot easier. All you need to do is prepare cat litter, balls of yarn, and some paper boxes. Unlike dogs, cats are quieter, tidier, and more independent. Best of all, cats are natural born pest killers!

對我而言，比起狗，我更愛貓。雖然我不否認我身旁養狗的朋友比養貓的多，不過貓的確有些特質在狗身上是找不到。就我朋友的經驗，照顧貓簡單多了。你只需要準備貓砂、幾球毛線和一些紙箱即可。像狗，貓比較安靜、比較愛整潔、且個性比較獨立。最棒的是，貓還是天生的害蟲殺手呢！

重點補充

如果你對貓或狗沒什麼感覺，也可以說自己並不是愛狗或愛貓人士，並說明為什麼對這些動物沒什麼感覺，或是提到自己最喜歡的其他動物也是可行的。

I'm not a dog person or cat person. I don't have special feelings to cats and dogs, but I like Guinea pigs. They are so adorable and chubby. Sometimes I wish I can keep a guinea pig as a pet, but I need to get more information about how to take care of a Guinea pig.

我並不是愛狗或愛貓人士，我對貓、狗沒有特別的感覺，但是我喜歡天竺鼠。牠們非常可愛又圓滾滾的。有時候我希望我能養一隻天竺鼠當寵物，但我需要有更多關於如何照顧天竺鼠的資訊。

9 Do you agree that money is everything? Why or why not?

你同意錢是萬能的嗎？為什麼同意或為什麼不同意？

答題策略

這題包含了兩個問題，因此首先要回答自己對錢的觀點是什麼，要提到你認為有錢就可以完成很多事情，或是覺得錢財是身外之物，講完自己的觀點後，則要說明自己為什麼會這樣認為，才能形成完整的論述。

回答範例 1

Maybe you would say I'm a mammonist, but I must admit that money talks. Of course one might argue that money can't buy happiness or health, while there are some things that need to be done with money to make us happy or healthy. For example, a rich patient will get high-end medical treatment for recovery as long as he or she can afford it. Nevertheless, I don't mean money is the most important; I just feel that there is almost nothing in the world we can get for free.

也許你會說我很拜金，但我必須承認金錢是萬能的。當然可能會有人反駁，說金錢無法買到快樂或健康，不過有些事情需要用錢來完成，才能讓我們快樂或健康。比如說

一位有錢的病人，只要他負擔得起費用，為了痊癒就能夠得到高級的醫藥治療。儘管如此，我並不是指金錢是最重要的，我只是覺得世界上幾乎沒有什麼東西是可以免費到手的。

It's out of the question. If money is everything, why are there still some rich people who commit crimes or have depression? Having everything doesn't mean one is satisfied spiritually. I read a study which said money can only meet basic human needs whereas there is no evidence to imply that being richer equals being happier. There are things on earth that can't be replaced with money, such as family, true love, and inner peace.

這是不可能的。如果金錢是萬能的，為什麼有些富人仍會犯罪或患有憂鬱症？擁有一切不代表這個人精神上是滿足的。我讀過一篇研究，提到金錢只能滿足人類基本需求，不過沒有證據能暗示越有錢等於越快樂。這世界上有一些無法用金錢取代的東西，比如家庭、真愛、及內心平靜。

10　You get up one day feeling unwell, and you're about to leave a message to your teacher through voicemail. What will you say to him or her?

有一天起床你發現身體不舒服，並準備用語音信箱留言給老師。你會對他／她說什麼呢？

答題策略

這題先設定了一個情境，要你試著帶入情境中的角色來回答，因此在回答時要想像自己請病假時應該要說些什麼。首先，要跟老師打招呼，再說出自己生病了、有什麼症狀，並跟老師說後續你會做什麼事情，讓老師不用為你擔心，這種情況用英文表達就是（keep sb. posted）。

回答範例 1

Morning, Mr. Huang. It's Joe. I'm sorry, but I won't be able to come to school today. I had diarrhea this morning and I'm still feeling weak. I guess I might have had something bad for my dinner yesterday. I'll go to a doctor later and get a proof for you these days. By the way, I've asked Rita to cover for me since I'm the helper of history. I'll be back to school tomorrow and keep up with the lessons for today.

黃老師早安，我是 Joe。很抱歉，我今天無法去上學。我早上拉肚子，目前仍感到很虛弱。我猜可能是我昨天晚餐吃了不乾淨的東西，我待會會去看醫生，然後這幾天拿診斷證明給您。對了，因為我是歷史課的小老師，我已經請 Rita 暫代我的職位。我明天會回學校，並且跟上今天沒上到的課程。

回答範例 2

Hi, Ms. Smith. It's me, Emily. I need to take a few days off. I've been coming down with the unexpected flu since last night. I took an aspirin but it was not working; worse still, I've got a rash all over and a high fever. I'm feeling extremely drowsy now and I could use some rest. My mom said she'll make an appointment with the doctor for me around eight-thirty. I'll keep you posted as soon as possible.

嗨，Smith 老師。是我，Emily。我需要請幾天假。我昨晚開始突然得流感，吃了一顆阿斯匹靈，但沒有效用；更糟的是，我全身還長疹子和發高燒。我現在整個人超睏，需要休息一下。我媽媽說她幫我預約八點半左右的門診，我看情況如何會盡快跟您說明。

下面有一張圖片及四個相關的問題,請在 1 分半鐘內完成作答。作答時,請直接回答,不需將題號及題目唸出。

首先請利用 30 秒的時間看圖及問題。

 1. 照片裡的人在什麼地方?
2. 照片裡的人在做什麼?
3. 照片裡的人為什麼會在那裡?
4. 如果尚有時間,請詳細描述圖片中的景物。

草稿擬定

1. 照片裡的人在什麼地方?公共場合 public places、廣場 square
2. 照片裡的人身上有什麼、在做什麼?服裝 costume、街頭藝人 street artist、樂器 musical instrument、電吉他 electric guitar
3. 照片裡的人為什麼會在那裡?表演 perform、提供娛樂 provide entertainment、報償 reward、觀眾 audience
4. 如果尚有時間,請詳細描述與圖片相關的情境。街頭藝人的表演形式 street artist performance style

高分 SOP

照片中的主角是彈電吉他的人，請把敘述內容的焦點放在這個人身上。建議先從照片的拍攝地點開始講，這個人在什麼地方？你看到什麼？記得不要一次說完，要把觀察到的事物一層一層地說明，讓整個敘述更清晰。例如先說「這是在白天的戶外拍攝的，我可以看到有位男士在廣場人群面前彈著電子吉他。他穿得很休閒，包括鴨舌帽、一件夾克、牛仔褲及靴子」。照片中可以說的都說完了，可以加入自己的看法。對街頭藝人的看法是什麼？街頭藝人有什麼表演型態呢？這些都可以加到自己的敘述中。

必殺萬用句

1. Well, what can I say about this picture?（嗯，關於這張照片我該說什麼呢？）
   遇到一時之間腦袋一片空白的情況，可以用這句來佔一些時間。
2. Although I can only see..., I guess...（雖然我只能看到…，我猜…）
   照片呈現的內容有限，因此用 I guess 來表達自己所猜想的情境。
   Although I can only see the back of him, I guess he must enjoy what he is doing.
   （雖然我只能看到他的背影，但我猜他一定很享受他正在做的事情。）
3. Like many others around the world, ...（跟世界各地的其他人一樣，…。）
   後面可以加上其他跟圖片有關的例子，讓整個敘述的內容更豐富。
4. I have to admit that...（我必須承認…）
   因為圖片跟街頭藝人的表演有關，可以用這個句型，加上自己對街頭藝人印象深刻的想法。

Well, what can I say about this picture? It was taken outside in the daytime. I can see a man playing the electric guitar in front of people on the square. He is casually dressed, including a cap, a jacket, jeans and boots. Although I can only see the back of him, I guess he must enjoy what he is doing. In the background are the audience gathering around to hear the man play music. They might be standing in a circle, paying attention to his performance. The guitar case, opened and placed on the ground, is used for collecting money as a reward from the audience. Like many others around the world, the man in the picture is known as a street artist, who shows his talent in public places. Some would do the singing or dancing. Others would perform magic tricks such as playing cards or juggling. Still others would just pose themselves like a living statue. I have to admit that some of their street performances are really impressive and breathtaking.

範例中譯

嗯，關於這照片我該怎麼說呢？這是在白天的戶外拍攝的，我可以看到有名男子在廣場的人群面前彈著電吉他。他穿得很休閒，包括鴨舌帽、一件夾克、牛仔褲及靴子。雖然我只能看到他的背影，但我猜他一定很享受他正在做的事情。照片背景有一群圍觀的觀眾，他們聆聽這位男子彈奏的音樂，他們可能圍成一圈並專心看他的表演。地上放著一個打開的吉他箱，它是用來裝觀眾打賞的金錢。跟世界各地其他人一樣，照片這位男子也就是我們熟知的街頭藝人，他們會在公共場合表演才藝。有人唱歌跳舞、有人表演變魔術像是玩牌或作雜耍、有人就乾脆把自己扮演活雕像。我必須承認，有些街頭表演真的讓人印象深刻且嘆為觀止。

第六回　寫作能力測驗答題注意事項

1. 本測驗共有兩部分。第一部分為中譯英，第二部分為英文作文。測驗時間為 **40 分鐘**。

2. 請利用試題紙空白處背面擬稿，但正答務必書寫在「寫作能力測驗答案紙」上。在答案紙以外的地方作答，不予計分。

3. 第一部分中譯英請在答案紙第一頁作答，第二部分英文作文請在答案紙第二頁作答。

4. 作答時請勿隔行書寫，請注意字跡清晰可讀，並保持答案紙之清潔，以免影響評分。

5. 測驗時，不得在准考證或其他物品上抄題，亦不得有傳遞、夾帶小抄、左顧右盼或交談等違規行為。

6. 意圖或已經將試題紙攜出試場者，五年內不得報名參加本測驗。請人代考者，連同代考者，三年內不得報名參加本測驗。

7. 測驗結束時，須立即停止作答，在原位靜候監試人員收回全部試題紙及答案紙，清點無誤後，宣佈結束始可離場。

8. 應試者入場、出場及測驗中如有違反上列規則或不服監試人員之指示者，監試人員得取消應試資格並請其離場，且作答不予計分。

全民英語能力分級檢定測驗

中級寫作能力測驗

本測驗共有兩部份。第一部份為中譯英，第二部份為英文寫作。測驗時間為 40 分鐘。

一、中譯英 (40%)

說明：請將下列的一段中文翻譯成通順、達意且前後連貫的英文。

新冠肺炎這幾年讓全世界的人措手不及，很多年長者被感染後因而死亡。目前許多國家正提供不同種類的疫苗讓人民使用，台灣也不例外。跟許多其他人一樣，我也在等待疫苗中，但我知道至少目前可以做的是戴口罩、勤洗手及外出時保持安全距離。

二、英文作文 (60%)

請依下面所提供的文字提示寫一篇英文作文，長度約 120 字（8 至 12 個句子）。作文可以是一個完整的段落，也可以分段。（評分重點包括內容、組織、文法、用字遣詞、標點符號、大小寫。）

提示：英文是國際語言，台灣這幾年也在積極推動全英語課程；你對全英語上課的看法為何？請以此為題，寫一篇英文作文。

1. 描述你目前觀察到的英語教學現況。
2. 說明你是否贊成全英語上課及理由。

第一部份請由第 1 行開始作答，請勿隔行書寫。　　　　　　第 1 頁

5

10

15

20

25

30

35

40

第六回　口說能力測驗答題注意事項

1. 本測驗問題由耳機播放，回答則經麥克風錄下。分朗讀短文、回答問題與看圖敘述三部分，時間共約 15 分鐘，連同口試說明時間共需約五十分鐘。

2. 第一部份朗讀短文有 1 分鐘準備時間，此時請勿唸出聲音，待聽到「請開始朗讀」2 分鐘的朗讀時間開始時，再將短文唸出來。第二部分回答問題的題目將播出 2 遍，聽完第二次題目後要立即回答。第三部份看圖敘述有 30 秒的思考時間及 1 分 30 秒的答題時間，思考時不可在試題紙上作記號，亦不可出聲。等聽到指示開始回答時，請您針對圖片盡量的回答。

3. 錄音設備皆已事先完成設定，請勿觸動任何機件，以免影響錄音。測驗時請戴妥耳機，將麥克風調到嘴邊約三公分處，聽清楚說明，依指示以適中音量回答。

4. 評分人員將根據您錄下的回答（發音與語調、語法與字彙、可解度及切題度等）作整體的評分。您可利用所附光碟自行測試，一一錄下回答後，再播出來聽聽，並斟酌調整。練習時請盡量以英語思考、應對，考試時較易有自然的表現。

5. 請注意測試時不可在試題紙上劃線、打「√」或作任何記號；不可在准考證或其他物品上抄題；亦不可有傳遞、夾帶小抄、左顧右盼或交談等違規行為。

6. 意圖或已將試題紙或試題影音資料攜出或傳送出試場者，視同侵犯本中心著作財產權，限五年內不得報名參加「全民英檢」測驗。請人代考，連同代考者，三年內不得報名參加本測驗。

7. 測驗結束時，須立即停止作答，在原位靜候監試人員收回全部試題紙且清點無誤後，等候監試人員宣布結束後始可離場。

8. 入場、出場及測驗中如有違反規則或不服監試人員指示者，監試人員將取消您的應試資格並請您離場，且作答不予計分，亦不退費。

全民英語能力分級檢定測驗

中級口說能力測驗

請在 15 秒內完成並唸出下列自我介紹的句子：

My seat number is（座位號碼後 5 碼）, and my registration number is（考試號碼後 5 碼）.

第一部分：朗讀短文

請先利用一分鐘的時間閱讀下面的短文，然後在二分鐘內以正常的速度，清楚正確的讀出下面的短文，閱讀時請不要發出聲音。

Over the decades, Internet terms have created new vocabulary for us, but they have also reflected personal values and manners for the society. Take the following words, *ghosting* and *zombieing*, for example, they are used nowadays to describe the situation in which someone disappears for no reason after chatting with others online, showing that the person might fear face-to-face interactions. In a sense, we can take these terms as a "mirror" to see who we are becoming in the cyber world.

*　　　　　　　*　　　　　　　*

Despite the fact that Pixar and Disney are both excellent at making world-famous animations, there are a few differences between the two. According to the previous studies and online survey, Pixar's animated films are recognized as more original and better received than Disney's, whether by critics or by audiences. Nonetheless, Disney tops Pixar in terms of the overall box office. This is most obvious when its blockbusters *Snow White* and *Frozen* took the world by storm.

第二部分：回答問題

這個部分共有 10 題。題目已事先錄音，每題經由耳機播出二次，不印在試卷上。第一至五題，每題回答時間 15 秒；第六至十

題，每題回答時間 30 秒。每題播出後，請立即回答。回答時，不一定要用完整的句子，但請在作答時間內儘量的表達。

第三部分：看圖敘述

下面有一張圖片及四個相關的問題，請在一分半鐘內完成作答。作答時，請直接回答，不需將題號及題目唸出。

首先請利用 30 秒的時間看圖及問題。

提示：
1. 照片裡的人在什麼地方？
2. 照片裡的人在做什麼？
3. 照片裡的人為什麼會在那裡？
4. 如果尚有時間，請詳細描述圖片中的景物。

請將下列自我介紹的句子再唸一遍：

My seat number is（座位號碼後 5 碼）, and my registration number is（考試號碼後 5 碼）.

複試 寫作測驗 解析

▶▶▶ 第一部分 中譯英 (40%)

請將下列的一段中文翻譯成通順、達意且前後連貫的英文。

新冠肺炎這幾年讓全世界的人措手不及，很多年長者被感染後因而死亡。目前許多國家正提供不同種類的疫苗讓人民使用，台灣也不例外。跟許多其他人一樣，我也在等待疫苗中。但我知道至少目前可以做的是戴口罩、勤洗手及外出時保持安全距離。

翻譯範例

COVID-19 has caught people worldwide off guard over the years, while a lot of senior citizens died of infection. At present, many countries are providing different kinds of vaccines for their people; Taiwan is no exception. Like many others, I am waiting for the vaccines, too. However, at least what I can do is to wear a mask, wash my hands often, and keep a safe distance when going out.

逐句說明

1. 新冠肺炎這幾年讓全世界的人措手不及，很多年長者被感染後因而死亡。

COVID-19 has caught people worldwide off guard over the years, while a lot of senior citizens died of infection.

　　這題的翻譯和時事有關，因此考生在翻譯時需要知道許多與新冠肺炎相關的單字，才能寫出正確的翻譯。首先，新冠肺炎普遍的名稱是「Covid-19」，而「讓人措手不及」可以用「catch people off guard」來表達。另外，「感染後死亡」可以轉換成「die of infection」，意思是死於感染。

2. 目前許多國家正提供不同種類的疫苗讓人民使用，台灣也不例外。

At present, many countries are providing different kinds of vaccines for their people; Taiwan is no exception.

「目前」在英文中有許多表達，例如：presently、currently、at present 等。另外要注意的是，疫苗的英文是「vaccine」，若不知道怎麼寫出疫苗的英文，就沒辦法翻出正確的意思，而被扣分。最後「不例外」的英文可以用片語「no exception」來表達。

3. 跟許多其他人一樣，我也在等待疫苗中。

Like many others, I am waiting for the vaccines, too.

這句很容易就能翻譯出來，但要注意的地方是，這句的英文翻譯要用現在進行式，因為「我也在等待疫苗中」表示這件事仍在進行中。另外，「等待某件事」的英文可以用「wait for sth.」來表達。

4. 但我知道至少目前可以做的是戴口罩、勤洗手及外出時保持安全距離。

However, at least what I can do is to wear a mask, wash my hands often, and keep a safe distance when going out.

在寫英文的作文或翻譯時，為了避免句子不連貫，人們會使用一些連接句子的副詞來讓句子更通順。這裡可以用「however」來翻譯「但」，並在後面加上逗號。而「至少」的英文表達則是「at least」，而「我可以做的是」則可以用「What I can do is...」來表達，「保持安全距離」則是用「keep a safe distance」來表示。

第1回
第2回
第3回
第4回
第5回
第6回

請依下面所提供的文字提示寫一篇英文作文，長度約 120 字（8 至 12 個句子）。作文可以是一個完整的段落，也可以分段。

提示 英文是國際語言，台灣這幾年也在積極推動全英語課程；你對全英語上課的看法為何？請以此為題，寫一篇英文作文。

1. 描述你目前觀察到的英語教學現況。
2. 說明你是否贊成全英語上課及理由。

結構預設

這題作文的題目與教育有關，要提出考生目前所觀察到的台灣英語教學情況，以及自己對全英語授課的看法，並提出自己贊成或反對的理由。建議第一句可以寫有許多國家很重視學習英語，之後引導出台灣政府針對學習英語的情況。

草稿擬定

1. 開場白：文章一開始可以提到學習英語在世界各地的**趨勢**，因此可以用 Learning English 當作開頭，並在後面引導出學習英語是許多國家必要的事物。
2. 文章可以分成兩個段落，第一段從世界學習英語的**趨勢**，再談到台灣人學習英語的情況為何。
3. 第二段再提到自己對全英語授課的看法是什麼，贊成、部分贊成、反對或是完全反對，並且還要說出合理的原因。提出自己的看法可以用 In my opinion、personally 等片語、副詞來表達。

Learning English is a ①must in many countries. Over the years, our government has been ②making efforts to turn Taiwan into a ③bilingual nation, hoping that it will be more competitive in the future. In Taiwan, ④some teachers prefer both English and Chinese in class, while others insist on English-only classrooms. English is taught in various approaches.

⑤Personally, I do not see the English-only thing suits people in Taiwan. If allowed to use only English in class, low-level students would find it so hard to ⑥keep up with the lessons that they may as well give up in the end. ⑦In such cases, it must ⑧widen the gap between good learners and poor ones. Therefore, teaching partly in English would let most students feel less anxious over learning.

範例中譯

學英語在許多國家是必要的事。這幾年來，我們的政府一直努力將台灣轉變成雙語國家，希望在未來會更有競爭力。在台灣，有些老師偏好在課堂上用中、英文這兩種語言上課，然而有些老師則堅持在課堂全英語上課。英語可以用各式各樣的方法來教學。

就個人而言，我不認為全英語這件事適合台灣人。如果在課堂上只使用英文，那麼程度差的學生就會覺得很難跟上進度，以致最後可能就乾脆放棄了。在這樣的情形下，勢必會讓程度好與不好的學習者落差更大。因此，用部分英語授課才能讓大多數的學生在學習上不會感到那麼焦慮。

重點文法分析

① 一般人比較熟悉 must 當助動詞的用法，然而 must 當名詞時意思是「必須做的事」，用在平常的表達時，會說 doing something is a must，代表做這件事是必要的。

② making efforts to V 指的是「努力去做某件事」，另外也可以改成「make every effort to V」，這是指「竭盡所能去做某件事」的意思。

③ bilingual 這個詞彙的意思是「雙語的；懂兩種語言的」，而 monolingual 的意思是「單語的」、multilingual 的意思則是「懂多種語言的」。

④ Some+ V..., while others + V... 這個句型可以用在對比的情況下，指的是「有些人喜歡做…，而其他人則喜歡做…」

⑤ Personally, 這個副詞的意思是「就個人而言」，通常在作文中會放在句子的開頭，並在後面加上自己的看法。

⑥ keep up with 的意思是「保持在同一個速度；跟上…」，可以用來表達跟上…的趨勢或是進度。

⑦ In such cases, 指的是「在這樣的情形下」，在寫文章時，前面可能提到某種特殊的情況，後面的句子可以加上 in such cases, 並且寫出這種情形可能發生的結果。

⑧ widen the gap between A and B 指的是「使 A 和 B 之間的差距擴大」，而在例文中則是表達程度差的同學和其他同學之間的差距擴大。

複試 口說測驗 解析

▶▶▶ 第一部分 朗讀短文

> 請先利用 1 分鐘的時間閱讀下面的短文，然後在 2 分鐘內以正常的速度，清楚正確的讀出下面的短文。

 短文

Over the decades, Internet terms have created new vocabulary for us, but they have also reflected personal values and manners for the society. Take the following words, *ghosting* and *zombieing*, for example, they are used nowadays to describe the situation in which someone disappears for no reason after chatting with others online, showing that the person might fear face-to-face interactions. In a sense, we can take these terms as a "mirror" to see who we are becoming in the cyber world.

*　　　　　　　*　　　　　　　*

Despite the fact that Pixar and Disney are both excellent at making world-famous animations, there are a few differences between the two. According to the previous studies and online survey, Pixar's animated films are recognized as more original and better received than Disney's, whether by critics or by audiences. Nonetheless, Disney tops Pixar in terms of the overall box office. This is most obvious when its blockbusters *Snow White* and *Frozen* took the world by storm.

這幾十年來，網路術語已經為我們創造新的詞彙，但這些詞彙也反映出個人價值觀及對社會的態度。以 ghosting 及 zombieing 為例，這些詞目前被用來描述某個人在網路跟人聊天後卻莫名搞失蹤的情況，顯示出這個人可能害怕面對面互動。就某種意義上來說，我們可以將這些術語視為「鏡子」，以檢視我們在網路世界所成為的角色。

*　　　　　　　　*　　　　　　　　*

雖然皮克斯跟迪士尼都擅長製作世界有名的動畫片，這兩者之間仍有一些差異。根據之前的研究及網路調查的結果，皮克斯動畫被認可比迪士尼的還具有原創性及評價更好，不論以影評或觀眾的立場。儘管如此，迪士尼在總票房上則超越了皮克斯。從它這兩部席捲全球的賣座鉅片《白雪公主》及《冰雪奇緣》來看更是明顯。

1 重要單字：decade [ˋdɛked] 十年；vocabulary [vəˋkæbjəˌlɛrɪ] 字彙；personal [pɝsn̩l] 個人的；manner [ˋmænə] 態度；zombieing [ˋzɑmbɪŋ] 突然消失又突然出現；nowadays [ˋnɑʊəˌdez] 現今；disappear [ˌdɪsəˋpɪr] 消失；interaction [ˌɪntəˋrækʃən] 互動；cyber [ˋsɑɪbə] 電腦的、網路的；excellent [ˋɛksl̩ənt] 傑出的；animation [ˌænəˋmeʃən] 動畫片；previous [ˋpriviəs] 之前的；survey [səˋve] 調查；recognize [ˋrɛkəgˌnɑɪz] 承認；critic [ˋkrɪtɪk] 評論家；nonetheless [ˌnʌnðəˋlɛs] 然而；blockbuster [ˋblɑkˌbʌstə] 大轟動

2 請注意有些詞彙的母音發音是長母音還是短母音，例如 previous 的 e 就是長母音，而不是短母音，而 survey 的 ey 也是長母音的 a，在朗讀時要多注意，才不會因為發成錯誤的音而被扣分。

3 朗讀高分技巧
以下朗讀文章中有顏色的單字需要唸稍微大聲一點，讓語調有起伏。文章中有 | 的地方表示可以稍做停頓，讓語氣更加從容，更有自信。

Over the decades, | Internet terms have created new vocabulary for us, | but they have also reflected | personal values and manners for the society. | Take the following words, | *ghosting* and *zombieing*, | for example, | they are used nowadays to describe the situation | in which someone disappears for no reason | after chatting with others online, | showing that the person might fear face-to-face interactions. | In a sense, | we can take these terms as a "mirror" | to see who we are becoming | in the cyber world.

*   *   *

Despite the fact that Pixar and Disney | are both excellent at making world-famous animations, | there are a few differences between the two. | According to the previous studies and online survey, | Pixar's animated films | are recognized as more original | and better received than Disney's, | whether by critics | or by audiences. | Nonetheless, | Disney tops Pixar | in terms of the overall box office. | This is most obvious | when its blockbusters *Snow White* and *Frozen* | took the world by storm.

▶▶▶ 第二部分 回答問題

> 這個部分共有 10 題。題目已事先錄音，每題經由耳機播出二次，不印在試卷上。第 1 至 5 題，每題回答時間 15 秒；第 6 至 10 題，每題回答時間 30 秒。每題播出後，請立即回答。回答時，不一定要用完整的句子，但請在作答時間內盡量的表達。

1   **What did you use to do when you were a kid?**
你小時候常做什麼事情？

這題是很好發揮的題目，回答時你可以提到自己的生長背景（住在城市或是鄉下），並且說自己小時候經常做的事情，例如喜歡玩什麼玩具、興趣、跟朋友做什麼活動等。

回答範例 1

There were so many things I did in my childhood. I used to play outdoor activities with my neighbors since my family lived in the countryside. We played tag, hide-and-seek, hopscotch, and sometimes Frisbee. I would say that was the best time in my life.

我童年時期做過許多事情了。因為我的家庭那時候住鄉下，我常跟鄰居們做戶外活動。我們那時候玩鬼抓人、捉迷藏、跳房子，有時候還會玩飛盤。我會說，那是我人生中最棒的時刻。

回答範例 2

Since I was little, I've made friends with cell phones because both my parents were computer engineers. I used to play Angry Birds, watch Sponge Bob, and even do homework on my cell phone. On top of that, I exchanged Pokémon action figures with my classmates, and I enjoyed it.

從我小時候起，我就跟手機做朋友，因為我爸媽當時都是電腦工程師。我以前會在手機上玩憤怒鳥、看海綿寶寶卡通、甚至做回家作業。除此之外，我會跟同學交換寶可夢公仔，而且我滿享受這樣的事。

重點補充

如果你的童年沒有做很多特別的事情，你也可以講小時候對你很重要的人，以及你跟他們相處的經驗。

Come to think of it, I can't remember much about my childhood. All I know is that I lived with my grandparents. They had a farm, and I played with those farm animals.

回頭想想，我對我的童年記得不多。我所知道的是，我跟我的爺爺、奶奶住在一起。他們有一個農場，而我會跟那些農場動物一起玩。

2 When was the last time you felt embarrassed? Tell us about your experience.

你最近何時發生讓你尷尬的事情？請和我們分享你的經驗。

答題策略

這題問的是自己發生過尷尬的事情，因此可以從自己的經驗來發想，不用提到太過複雜的事情，只要想在短時間可以回答完的事情就可以了。例如：在正式場合穿了不適當的服裝、或者把訊息傳給錯的人。

回答範例1

Last week I was invited to a party. I was told that it was just a simple get-together. I wore a blouse and jeans that day, but later I found that those at the party were either in an evening suit or in a cheongsam. I was so embarrassed that I left the party immediately.

上週我被邀請去參加一個派對，我被告知這只是個單純的聚會。我當天穿了一件（女）短上衣和牛仔褲，但之後我發現參加派對的人不是穿晚禮服就是旗袍。我尷尬到馬上就離開派對了。

回答範例2

My embarrassing moment was yesterday when my girlfriend and I were texting about the wedding. I sent "Will you marry me?" to her brother by accident. He sent back a sticker of facepalm and asked if my account was hacked. How I wanted the ground to open up and swallow me!

我尷尬的事情就發生在昨天，我當時跟女友互傳有關婚禮的訊息，我不小心把「妳願意嫁給我嗎？」的訊息傳到她弟弟那邊。他回傳一個無奈（手遮臉）的貼圖，還問我帳號是否被盜用了。我那時真希望有個地洞可以鑽進去！

Do men or women spend more money on shopping? Please explain.

你覺得男人還是女人花比較多錢在購物上？請解釋原因。

答題策略

這題是詢問自己對於男人和女人在購物方面的想法，可以說你認為男生會花比較多錢，或是女生會花比較多錢，但是要注意題目後面還有加上 please explain，因此除了說出自己的想法，也要提出背後的原因才會得到完整的分數。

回答範例 1

If the question here doesn't refer to shopping for outfits only, I guess the answer might be men. Men are more attracted to electronic devices than women. Males would rather spend money on something more expensive but with better quality than the other way around.

如果這個問題沒有只針對買衣服的話，我猜答案可能是男人。男人比女人更容易受到電子產品吸引，男性寧願花錢買較貴但品質較好的東西，而不願買相反的東西。

回答範例 2

I can't say for sure how much is spent on shopping by each gender, but I think women shop more often than men. However, women usually do this when it comes to group buying, big sales, coupons, and free samples. Women take shopping as an activity while men take it as a task.

我無法確定各個性別在購物上花費了多少，但我覺得女人比男人更常購物。不過，女人通常在團購、大特賣、優惠券及免費試用品時才會購物。女人把購物視為一項活動，而男人則把它視為一項任務。

重點補充

如果你認為男生、女生購物並沒有差別，你也可以用下列的敘述來回答。

It's hard to say. It depends on people's shopping habits. I think many people will spend their money on what they want to buy. Some people tend to buy more expensive products; while others prefer to save their money. It has nothing to do with their genders.

這很難說，這取決於人們的購物習慣。我想很多人會把錢花在他們想買的東西上。有些人傾向於購買更昂貴的產品；而其他人則偏好存錢。這與他們的性別無關。

4 **What animal do you think you were in a past life? Why?**

你覺得你上輩子是什麼動物？為什麼？

答題策略

這題的回答需要靠想像力，你必須決定要回答哪一種動物。因為題目有問為什麼，所以你要說出與這個動物的相似之處，可能是個性或習慣很相似、或是外表相似，只要回答出合理的原因，就能得到分數。另外前面可以說，這是一個有趣的問題，讓整個回答更順暢。

回答範例 1

Well, that's an interesting question, but if I have to give an answer off hand, I suppose I was an ant in my past life. I have a sweet tooth, keep early hours, and like to work with others. All these qualities make me feel that ants and I have something in common.

嗯，這是個有趣的問題，但如果我要馬上給答案的話，我想我上輩子應該是螞蟻。我愛吃甜食、早睡早起、而且喜歡跟他人共事。這些全部的特質都讓我覺得我跟螞蟻有一些共同之處。

For me personally, I might be a lion in my previous life. My parents said I was drawn to toy lions when I was little. My friends agree that I'm dominant, enjoy being myself, and have a sense of justice. I don't mean I'm proud to be like a lion; it's just I happen to be the way I am.

我個人覺得，我上輩子可能是獅子。我爸媽說我小時候會被玩具獅子吸引，我朋友都同意我個性強勢、喜歡做自己、又具有正義感。我並不是說像獅子讓我覺得自豪，只是我剛好是這樣的人。

5 Your friend Amy failed this GEPT test and she felt depressed. What would you say to her?

你的朋友 Amy 沒通過這次全民英檢考試，而且她很沮喪，你會對她說什麼？

答題策略

這題在回答前要讓自己先進入題目的情境中，思考自己如何安慰考試考不好的朋友，並把它套用在回答中。可以告訴朋友她已經盡力了，可以約出來散散心，或是請朋友針對自己在考試上的弱點請教老師等。

回答範例 1

Amy, are you all right? I've heard that you didn't pass the test, and I know you must feel sad now because you had been working so hard for this. What do you say if we meet sometime tomorrow afternoon? We can grab something to eat together and talk about the test.

Amy，妳還好嗎？我聽說妳沒通過這次的考試；我知道妳現在一定很傷心，因為妳很努力在準備這次的考試。我們明天下午找個時間見面，妳覺得如何呢？我們可以一起吃點東西，然後聊聊這次的考試。

回答範例 2

I'm a little surprised you failed the GEPT test, Amy, especially when English is up your alley. You even had an English tutor for this, so I assume you just choked up this time because of stress. I suggest you watch some movies for a diversion. Just call me if you need help.

Amy，妳這次全民英檢沒過讓我有點驚訝，尤其英文是妳的拿手項目。妳甚至為此還請了英文家教，所以我想妳這次考試只是因為壓力而失常。我建議妳看一些電影轉移注意力。如果妳需要協助，可以打給我。

6　When you get sick, will you choose prescription medicine or over-the-counter medicine? Why?

當你生病時，你會選擇處方藥還是成藥？為什麼？

答題策略

這題在回答前要先了解 prescription medicine 和 over-the-counter medicine 是什麼意思。prescription medicine（處方藥）是指需要經過醫生開立的藥物；而 over-the-counter medicine（成藥）則是指在藥局就可以買到的藥物。回答時要提到自己生病時會選擇哪種藥物，並且解釋其中的原因。

回答範例 1

There are both advantages and disadvantages of prescription medicine and over-the-counter medicine. I feel more secure to get medicine from doctors because they can keep track of my medical record to decide which medicine is better for me. Getting medicine from a pharmacy is riskier, since I can't get specific suggestions without diagnosis.

處方藥跟成藥都各有優缺點。我覺得到透過醫生拿藥會比較安心，因為醫生可以追蹤我的就醫紀錄來決定哪種藥比較適合我。到藥局買藥比較冒險，因為沒有透過診斷，就得不到具體的建議。

回答範例 2

It depends on what type of illness I have. For example, if I have a slight cold, I will get the medicine directly from a pharmacy. Over-the-counter medicine is easier to get and has the same effect. However, if I have severe symptoms such as high fever, then it's safer to get medicine from doctors because they're professional and know better about my physical condition.

這要看我的疾病類型而定。舉例來說，如果我有輕微感冒，我會直接到藥局買藥。成藥比較容易取得且有同樣的效果。然而，如果我有嚴重的症狀，比如發高燒，那麼請醫生開藥會比較安全，因為他們很專業，而且比較了解我的身體狀況。

7 Have you ever made up an excuse for being late for school or work? Tell us about your experience.

你曾因上學或上班遲到而找藉口嗎？請跟我們分享你的經驗。

答題策略

這題可以簡單提出自己遲到的經驗，這裡要注意的是題目有指定是上學或上班的遲到經驗，因此你只能從這兩個情境來回答，可以簡單提到自己為什麼遲到，並且談到遲到後的後果是什麼。

回答範例 1

Basically, I'm not one to be tardy for school. However, there was one time when I stayed up all night singing at a KTV with my friends. I forgot to set the alarm, so I was late for school the next day. I lied to my teacher that my alarm didn't go off. My teacher didn't blame me for this, but she gave me a suspicious look. I know I'm bad at making excuses and it won't happen again.

基本上，我不是一個上學會遲到的人。然而，有一次我跟一群朋友熬夜 KTV。我忘了設定鬧鐘，因此隔天上學遲到是理所當然的。我騙老師說我鬧鐘沒響。我的老師雖沒責怪我，但是她給了我一個懷疑的眼神。我知道我不善於找藉口，而且這件事不會再發生了。

回答範例 2

I know it's not right, but I must confess that I have a habit of making up excuses for being late for work. In truth, my house is two-hour drive from my office, so I was barely punctual. One day, I was so late that I had to make a new excuse. I told the boss that my nephew ate the papers and was sent to the hospital. He sneered and said it was okay, but the next day I got a pink slip from him.

我知道這樣不對，但我必須坦承我之前習慣上班遲到就找藉口。事實上，我家離公司要兩小時的車程，因此我很少準時上班。有一天，我整個大遲到，不得不找新的藉口。我告訴老闆，我姪子把我的文件吃了，然後被送到醫院。他冷笑說沒關係；但隔天我就收到他發的解僱通知了。

重點補充

如果你是守時的人，你秉持著拿全勤獎的精神，並且不能接受自己或其他人遲到，你也可以用以下的敘述來回答。

I think to be on time is a sign of respect. If you are serious to your job or schoolwork, you will be on time. Unless you are late for an unavoidable accident, there is no excuse to be late.

我認為守時是一種重視的表現。如果你對你的工作、學業很認真，你就會守時。除非你因為不可避免的意外而晚來，否則就沒有藉口遲到。

8

Do you prefer handmade gifts or store-bought gifts? Why?

你會偏好手作禮物還是現成的禮物？為什麼？

答題策略

這題總共要回答的項目有兩個，第一個項目是傾向手作的還是現成的禮物，而第二個項目則是要說明喜歡這種禮物的原因。因此回答時要提到自己的傾向是什麼，之後則是回答其中的原因。若選擇手作的禮物可以說，這代表送禮者的心意；而選擇現成禮物可以回答，這種禮物比較方便，也讓送禮的過程更有效率。

回答範例 1

It depends on whether I'm a gift giver or a receiver. If I'm the giver, I will choose store-bought gifts because I'm really clumsy in doing arts and crafts. Store-bought gifts may not be my first choice, but at least they look decent. While, I prefer to get handmade gifts if I'm the receiver. How sweet it would be when someone is willing to make a gift for me, regardless of how it looks.

這要看我是送禮者還是收禮者。如果我是送禮的人，我會選擇現成的禮物，因為我在做手工藝上相當笨拙。現成的禮物也許不是我送禮的首選，但起碼它們看起來體面。然而如果我是收禮者，我會偏好收到手作禮物。當有人願意為我製作禮物時，這感覺多貼心；不管這禮物看起來如何。

回答範例 2

Although handmade gifts may not be as trendy as store-bought ones, most people choose the former over the latter. For instance, I planned to send a store-bought gift to a friend for her help last week, but I ended up making a thank-you card as a token of my appreciation. She said the card means a lot to her because it's one of a kind. Indeed, we always care so much about the value of gifts instead of the thought behind gift giving.

雖然手作禮物也許沒有店裡買的來得有型，但大多數的人會選前者勝過後者。舉個例子，我原本計畫要買禮物送一個朋友，因為她上週幫我一些忙；但最後我自己做一張感謝卡表示謝意。她說這張卡片對她意義重大，因為它是獨一無二的。的確，我們總是太在意禮物的價值，反而忽略了送禮背後的心意。

9 Do you believe in fortune telling? Why or why not?

你相信算命嗎？為什麼信或為什麼不信？

答題策略

這題需要仔細思考後再來回答，首先要說明自己是否相信算命，接下來要回答自己相信或不相信的原因。如果你相信算命，可以回答你相信很多事情都由命運來安排等原因；如果你不相信算命，則可以回答算命是一種迷信，很多事情還是要靠自己來掌握。

回答範例 1

Call me superstitious, but I really believe that our fate is written in the stars, and only fortune tellers can foresee what will happen in the future. They seem to be connected with some mysterious force that might have mapped out our destiny. That being said, I don't think that all fortune tellers are able to precisely predict everything about the unknown, such as the winning numbers for a lottery.

就說我迷信吧，但我真的相信命運冥冥中自有安排，而且只有算命師可以預知未來會如何。他們似乎跟某種神祕力量有所連結，而且這股力量可能已經規劃好我們的命運。儘管如此，我不認為所有算命師都有辦法精準預測所有未知的事，比如樂透的中獎號碼。

第 1 回
第 2 回
第 3 回
第 4 回
第 5 回
第 6 回

回答範例 2

Like astrology and supernatural powers, fortune telling is just another form of superstition since there is no scientific evidence in it. I know there are a number of cases in history where someone's prophecy about an event has come true. However, these are mere coincidences and I take them with a grain of salt. While some people would turn to fortune tellers for a sense of security, I always believe that the future is in our own hands.

如同占星術跟超自然能力，算命只是另一種形式的迷信，因為它並沒有任何科學證據。我知道歷史上有一些一語成讖的例子，不過那些只是純屬巧合，而且我都對它們持保留的態度。當有些人會為了求心安而找算命師，我則始終相信未來掌握在我們自己的手裡。

10 What is your life motto? Please explain why.
你的人生座右銘是什麼？請解釋原因。

答題策略

這題在回答前要先想好一句對自己有影響的至理名言，可以是一句簡短的名言或是電影台詞，接下來則要提到這句話為什麼會對自己這麼重要，或是這句話對自己的職場、生活態度有什麼樣的改變。

回答範例 1

As a school teacher, I need to pass the conduct of life on to my students. Still, there were many times at school when my efforts turned into a total failure however hard I'd tried. One day, my friend sent me a teacher's day card which said, "Students don't care how much you know until they know how much you care." The sentence really pulled me out of the darkness. I've changed my attitude towards students since then, and miraculously, we've been turning the corner these months!

身為學校的老師，我必須要傳達做人處事的道理給學生。不過，我在學校已有好幾次遇到怎麼努力都白費的情況。有一天，我的朋友送我一張教師節卡片，上面寫著：「學生不在乎你有多少知識，直到他們了解你有多在乎他們。」這句話當時真的把我從黑暗中拉了回來。我從那時候起就改變對學生的態度，而且出乎意料地，在這幾個月我們的關係正逐漸改善中！

回答範例 2

I didn't have a personal motto until I watched the movie *Forrest Gump* years ago. Upon hearing the line "Life is like a box of chocolates; you never know what you're gonna get," I kept the word in mind immediately. I don't like surprises, but I have to admit that things happen unexpectedly and sometimes it's needed to play it by ear. It's time to step out of my comfort zone and open myself up to new possibilities in life.

我之前並沒有自己的座右銘，直到我在幾年前看了一部電影《阿甘正傳》。當我聽到「人生就像一盒巧克力，你永遠不會知道會拿到哪一塊」這句台詞時，我馬上就記住了。我並不喜歡驚喜，但我必須承認事情常出乎意料，而且有時候需要隨機應變。是時候該是踏出我的舒適圈，並且放開心胸嘗試新事物的時候了。

下面有一張圖片及四個相關的問題，請在 1 分半鐘內完成作答。作答時，請直接回答，不需將題號及題目唸出。

首先請利用 30 秒的時間看圖及問題。

提示
1. 照片裡的人在什麼地方？
2. 照片裡的人在做什麼？
3. 照片裡的人為什麼會在那裡？
4. 如果尚有時間，請詳細描述圖片中的景物。

草稿擬定

1. 照片裡的人在什麼地方？補習班 cram school、教室 classroom、白板 white board、教具 teaching aids
2. 照片裡的人是誰？教師 teacher、學生 students
3. 照片裡的人為什麼會在那裡？上英文課 having an English class、問問題 asking questions
4. 如果尚有時間，請詳細描述圖片中的景物，以及自己的看法。給予獎勵 giving rewards、非常投入 very involved with sth.

必殺萬用句

1. I am pretty sure that this picture was taken in a...（我很確定這張照片是在⋯拍的。）
2. 空間 + is equipped with + 事物（這個空間有⋯的配備），可以形容照片中的地點有什麼樣的事物。
3. Judging from..., I suppose...（從⋯來判斷，我認為⋯），可以這個句型來表達自己從照片中的細節所聯想出的觀點。
4. It is evident that...（很明顯的是⋯），可以用這個句型來表達照片中很醒目的重點，讓敘述更加豐富。

回答範例

I am pretty sure that this picture was taken in a cram school. There are five people in the picture, including a female teacher and four students. The classroom is equipped with a couple of teaching aids. The one on the right is a poster about weather types and is taped to an easel. In the middle is a whiteboard with an eraser and some magnets. The sentence pattern "My name is…" has been written on the board, so they're most likely having an English class. On the left is a picture of the flag of the United Kingdom pasted on the wall. The students have their textbooks and stationery on the desks for the class. The teacher is asking some question while the students are eager to answer it by raising their hands. Judging from their interactions, I suppose the English teacher might be giving some rewards for their good work. It's evident that all of them are very involved with doing English activities.

範例中譯

我很確定這張照片是在一間補習班拍的。照片中有五個人，包括一位女老師及四位學生。教室備有幾項教具，右邊有一張關於天氣類型的海報，同時被貼在畫架上；中間的是一塊白板，附一個板擦和一些磁鐵。「我的名字是⋯」這個句型已經被寫在板子上了，所以他們很有可能在上英文課；

左邊貼在牆上的是一張英國國旗的圖片，學生的桌上有上課用的課本及文具。老師正在問問題，同時學生們正舉手搶答。從他們的互動來看，我想這位英文老可能正獎勵他們好的表現。很明顯地，所有人都很投入參與英文活動。

☆第一部分：中譯英

級分	分數	說明
5	40	翻譯能力佳 內容能充分表達題意；文段組織、連貫性甚佳，能充分掌握句型結構；用字遣詞、文法、拼字、標點及大小寫幾乎無誤。
4	32	翻譯能力可 內容適切表達題意；文段組織、連貫性及句子結構大致良好；用字遣詞、文法、拼字、標點及大小寫偶有錯誤，但不妨礙題意之表達。
3	24	翻譯能力有限 內容未能完全表達題意；文段結構鬆散，連貫性不足未能掌握句型結構；用字遣詞及文法時有錯誤，妨礙題意之表達，拼字、標點及大小寫也有錯誤。
2	16	稍具翻譯能力 僅能局部表達原文題意；文段組織不良並缺乏連貫性，句子結構掌握欠佳，大多難以理解；用字遣詞、文法、拼字、標點及大小寫錯誤嚴重。
1	8	無翻譯能力 內容無法表達題意；語句沒有結構概念及連貫性，無法理解；用字遣詞、文法、拼字、標點及大小寫之錯誤多且嚴重。
0	0	未答/等同未答

☆第二部分：英文作文

級分	分數	說明
5	60	**寫作能力佳** 內容適切表達題目要求，清楚有條理；組織甚佳；能靈活運用字彙及句型；文法、拼字或標點符號偶有錯誤。
4	48	**寫作能力可** 內容符合題目要求，大致清楚；組織大致完整；能正確運用字彙及句型；文法、拼字或標點符號雖有錯誤，但不影響理解。
3	36	**寫作能力有限** 內容大致符合題目要求，但未完全達意；組織尚可；字彙及句型掌握不佳；文法、拼字、標點符號錯誤偏多，影響理解。
2	24	**稍具寫作能力** 內容局部符合題目要求，大多難以理解；組織不良；能運用的字彙及句型有限；文法、拼字、標點符號有許多錯誤。
1	12	**無寫作能力** 內容未能符合題目要求，無法理解；缺乏組織；能運用的字彙及句型非常有限；文法、拼字、標點符號有過多錯誤。
0	0	未答/等同未答

級分	分數	說明
5	100	發音清晰、正確,語調正確、自然;對應內容切題,表達流暢;語法、字彙使用自如,雖仍偶有錯誤,但無礙溝通。
4	80	發音大致清晰、正確,語調大致正確、自然;對應內容切題,語法、字彙之使用雖有錯誤,但無礙溝通。
3	60	發音、語調時有錯誤,因而影響聽者對其語意的瞭解。已能掌握基本句型結構,語法仍有錯誤;且因字彙、片語有限,阻礙表達。
2	40	發音、語調錯誤均多,朗讀時常因缺乏辨識能力而略過不讀;因語法、字彙常有錯誤,而無法進行有效的溝通。
1	20	發音、語調錯誤多且嚴重,又因語法錯誤甚多,認識之單字片語有限,無法清楚表達,幾乎無溝通能力。
0	0	未答/等同未答。

學習筆記欄

學習筆記欄

新制多益

考前衝刺拿高分！

聽力、閱讀、單字全面提升

百萬考生唯一推薦的新制多益單字書！

不管題型如何變化，持續更新內容，準確度最高！

依 2018 年最新改版多益題型整理編排，滿足各種程度需求，學習更有效率！

定價：499 元

全新收錄完整 10 回聽力測驗試題

「題目本＋解析本」雙書裝、3 版本 MP3，做模擬測驗、複習單題、記單字，都好用！

讓最強多益破解機構 Hackers Academia 帶你快速提升解題能力、穩穩拿到黃金證書！

定價：880 元

全新收錄完整 10 回閱讀測驗

「題目本＋解析本」雙書裝、單字總整理線上音檔，精準模擬實際測驗、解答詳盡清楚！

讓最強多益破解機構 Hackers Academia 帶你快速提升解題能力、穩穩拿到黃金證書！

定價：880 元

台灣廣廈 國際出版集團
Taiwan Mansion International Group

國家圖書館出版品預行編目（CIP）資料

NEW GEPT 全新全民英檢中級寫作&口說題庫解析／國際語言中心委員會，
郭文興，陳鈺璽著. -- 初版. -- 新北市：國際學村, 2021.09
　面；　公分
ISBN 978-986-454-177-5（平裝附光碟片）
1.英語 2.作文 3.讀本

805.1892　　　　　　　　　　　　　　　　110012661

國際學村

NEW GEPT 全新全民英檢中級寫作&口說題庫解析【新制修訂版】
6回試題完全掌握最新內容與趨勢！完全符合英檢中級題型！

作　　　者／國際語言中心委員會、郭文興、陳鈺璽	編輯中心編輯長／伍峻宏・編輯／陳怡樺 封面設計／何偉凱・內頁排版／菩薩蠻數位文化有限公司 製版・印刷・裝訂／東豪・紘億・秉成

行企研發中心總監／陳冠蒨　　　媒體公關組／陳柔彣
　　　　　　　　　　　　　　　綜合業務組／何欣穎

發　行　人／江媛珍
法律顧問／第一國際法律事務所 余淑杏律師・北辰著作權事務所 蕭雄淋律師
出　　　版／國際學村
發　　　行／台灣廣廈有聲圖書有限公司
　　　　　　地址：新北市235中和區中山路二段359巷7號2樓
　　　　　　電話：（886）2-2225-5777・傳真：（886）2-2225-8052

代理印務・全球總經銷／知遠文化事業有限公司
　　　　　　地址：新北市222深坑區北深路三段155巷25號5樓
　　　　　　電話：（886）2-2664-8800・傳真：（886）2-2664-8801
郵政劃撥／劃撥帳號：18836722
　　　　　　劃撥戶名：知遠文化事業有限公司（※單次購書金額未滿1000元需另付郵資70元。）

■出版日期：2021年9月　　　　ISBN：978-986-454-177-5
　　　　　　2024年8月5刷　　版權所有，未經同意不得重製、轉載、翻印。